Praise for *[non]disclosure*

"A superb work! *[non]disclosure* by Renée D. Bondy speaks to us of the struggle of the individual to maintain hope in the face of institutional self-interest and actionable blindness. In her first novel, Bondy has accomplished something quite astonishing: a compelling meditation on the power of kindness told in an engrossing narrative with palpably real characters."

—André Narbonne, author of the Scotiabank Giller Prize–nominated *Lucien and Olivia*

"With a historian's thoughtful attention to context and detail and a storyteller's gift for evocation and immersion, Renée D. Bondy has composed a powerful narrative that pushes our horizons of understanding. These skills are married to the palpable spirit of a writer propelled by empathy, integrity, and love. In Bondy's hands, hope feels worth the risk."

—Susan Holbrook, author of *Ink Earl*

"A true masterclass on the power of solidarity and how community can either sustain us or drag us under. Equal parts gut-wrenching and beautiful, *[non]disclosure* is a powerful novel that sticks with you. A must-read."

—Julie S. Lalonde, author of *Resilience Is Futile: The Life and Death and Life of Julie S. Lalonde*

"Atmospheric."

—*Foreword Reviews*

# [NON]DISCLOSURE

a novel

Renée D. Bondy

Second Story Press

Library and Archives Canada Cataloguing in Publication

Title: [non]disclosure : a novel / Renée D. Bondy.
Other titles: Nondisclosure | Disclosure
Names: Bondy, Renée, author.
Identifiers: Canadiana (print) 2024032806X | Canadiana (ebook) 20240328086 | ISBN 9781772603927 (softcover) | ISBN 9781772604023 (EPUB)
Subjects: LCGFT: Novels.
Classification: LCC PS8603.O535 N66 2024 | DDC C813/.6—dc23


Edited by Liz Johnston
Cover design by Tree Abraham
Book design by Laura Atherton

Printed and bound in Canada

*Second Story Press gratefully acknowledges the support of the Ontario Arts Council and the Canada Council for the Arts for our publishing program. We acknowledge the financial support of the Government of Canada through the Canada Book Fund.*

Funded by the Government of Canada
Financé par le gouvernement du Canada | Canada



Published by
Second Story Press
20 Maud Street, Suite 401
Toronto, Ontario, Canada
M5V 2M5
www.secondstorypress.ca

*For victim-survivors.*

*And for my friend Charlene Senn,
whose research and activism make
the world a safer place for girls and
young women.*

"Most people misunderstand the crime of sexual abuse. They think of stolen youth, a child tucked under the arm and spirited away. But it isn't like someone entering your house and stealing something from you. Instead, someone leaves something with you that grows until it replaces you."

—Alexander Chee, "The Guardians,"
in *How to Write an Autobiographical Novel*

"In bearing witness, we're trying to correct a theft of power via a story. But power and stories, while deeply interconnected, are not the same things. One is rock, the other water. Over time, long periods of time, water always wins. What I want to know, even now, is: how?"

—Lacy Crawford, *Notes on a Silencing*

# [PART 1]

# [1969–1981]

My first memory is the taste of varnish. I was three, maybe four, standing on the kneeler with my lips resting on the pew in front of me. It smelled of wood and sweaty coins. I opened my mouth and scraped my teeth across the surface, and slivers of bitter varnish flaked off on my tongue. It was my secret, stealing those tiny wafers of yellow lacquer. No one knew.

Each Sunday, Mom, Dad, and I, and later my sister, Rachel, sat in the same pew, in the third row on the left. It was there I learned to genuflect and kiss my fingertips, to bless myself with lowered eyes and bowed head. I chanted along to prayers whose meanings I would never consider. The choir sang the same songs season after season, ancient psalms and dirges. I mouthed the words and used my finger to follow along in the hymnal, its spine broken from the weight of the lyrics. I thumbed through the pages and found the words *breast* and *ass* and *wretch*, and giggled.

I wore gloves and itchy tights and bows in my hair. My Sunday Best. I wore the same clothes every week, and church scents seeped into my coat. Candle wax and incense. Chrysanthemums and lilies. Brackish holy water. Dust. Brylcreem and unwashed clothing, toothpaste and stale breath. Wet boots warmed through the hour, and the smell of feet rose up. Perked coffee wafted from the basement before Communion, and my stomach growled for sugar donuts.

Dimes jingled in my pocket for the collection basket. Dimes for the missions, where the poor children in Africa went to school and learned about Jesus. Dimes for the Catholic Women's League. Dimes for the Right to Life group, who paced in front of the hospital carrying posters of bloody babies. Each year at Lent, I folded a Development and Peace box, a tiny cardboard bank to hold reparation for my sins. And each year, I forgot the box in the pew or took it home and left it on the kitchen counter.

I sat still and didn't move a muscle until I couldn't sit still anymore, and then I looked around as far as my neck would turn. In rows and rows of walnut pews sat families just like mine. Morning light through the stained-glass windows landed on their heads and shoulders in soft splotches of color. Gold, silver, blue, and pink murals covered the ceilings and walls. Alabaster saints and scholars high, high above the sanctuary, too many to count, looked down in judgment. Saint Francis was my favorite because little birds perched on his shoulders, like in the movie *Cinderella*. But I was fascinated by Saint Lucy, who offered her gouged out eyes on a plate.

The cathedral was the grandest building in the city by far, its opulence in contrast to the working-class homes and grubby factories that surrounded it. Only years later would I see its flaws: the hairline cracks in the gleaming walls and ceilings, ancient dust embedded in every crevice. Its crumbling foundation caused the building to creak and moan. Wind whistled through the stained-glass windows. Gold leaf flaked from the ceiling, and minute particles came to rest on the faithful. We breathed it in and it became part of us. I inhaled more than I exhaled.

Looking down from above the altar, a larger-than-life Jesus frowned in disappointment. Or perhaps in pity. *They do not know what they do*, he said, week after week. And nothing changed. *That's the beauty of it*, we were told. *The True Church*. Everything the same for two thousand years. Jesus' chest relaxed as he sighed, and his head lolled forward as he tried to lick his self-inflicted wounds.

I got bloody papercuts from the weekly bulletin, which I wore on my head like a hat on the way home. My dad smoked cigars in the car, and we all felt sick. One week, I vomited in the driveway, and the tiny flakes of varnish glistened in the sun.

Church was supposed to be the most important hour of the week, but it was just that: an hour. School and other events filled the rest of the week. In some ways, no-school days were easier since they were free, except for that hour at mass. But they could also feel too wide open, like a vast field that looked like it would take just a few minutes to cross but really took much longer.

Back then, children were seldom bored. We ran in packs like wild dogs. We rode our bicycles until our lungs burned. We threw rocks in the river and pretended they were bombs and waited for fish to rise to the surface. We poked the eyes out of dead fish on the shore. We dressed and undressed Barbie, then made a swimming pool for her from a green plastic dishpan so she could go skinny-dipping. We walked to the high school and threw a tennis ball against the brick wall. We watched reruns of *The Brady Bunch* and ate saltines smeared with butter and drank Kool-Aid. We roamed the house pretending to be invisible.

No-school days stretched out forever, but sometimes, they were interrupted by our parents' sudden demands. *Where are you going? Where have you been? Go outside and get some air! Come in and do your chores! It's time for dinner! When was the last time you had a bath? Where is your sister? Be in before dark!* Mostly though, adults didn't want to know exactly what we were doing, only that we were being good.

Being good was easy, or so we were told. *Be a good girl. Help your mother. Look out for your little sister. Get good grades. Clean your plate. Clean your room. Clean behind your ears. Clean, clean, clean.* Goodness was about what you did, but it could also be found deep inside if you just searched hard enough. We were sinners, but we were angels too. Sin could be washed away by goodness. It could be washed away in the bathtub, scoured with a face cloth. Even the stubborn stuff—between our toes, behind our ears, between our legs—could be scrubbed clean. Sin was no match for clean living.

At school, being good was about being quiet, knowing the answers, and sitting up straight. Good posture reflected good intent. It was easier to sit up straight in an unyielding church pew than at a desk. I sat as tall as I could, and the teacher beamed. I slid down, my right leg caught in the struts that bound the chair to the desk, and the teacher rolled her eyes and turned her back. I raised my hand when I knew the answer and sometimes when I didn't. *Pick me!*

I knew, we all knew, that to be chosen you had to be extra good. Ten percent of us were chosen ninety percent of the time. You could be chosen for being blond and rosy-cheeked, your hands and nails pink and smooth. Or for being smart as a whip, for knowing all the flash cards, and how to underline neatly with a ruler and red pencil. You might be chosen to boost your self-confidence, which didn't really need boosting. You were pinned with ribbons just for listening and saying *yes*.

You could also be chosen for being extra bad. If you day-dreamed and stared out the window, you were chosen for not paying attention and not knowing the answer. For fidgeting and dropping your pencil on the floor. For yawning during lessons. For picking at tattered hangnails and wiping snot on the cuff of your sweater. Once, a girl in our class stole milk from the lunch-room fridge. There was nothing to be done with her.

Sometimes, being chosen ran in the family. Goodness was often in the genes. You couldn't buy goodness, but you could inherit it. *Her sister was on the honor roll. His brother was captain of the basketball team. They're such a* good *family!* Of course, you could just as easily inherit badness and come up short. *Look what she comes from, poor thing. Remember her mother?*

But for all its rules and rituals, its judgments and favoritism, school was predictable. A shiny gold star on your spelling dictation paper. An F in penmanship. Pinned with a blue ribbon on Field Day. Your name on the board for speaking out. Praise and shame doled out in equal parts.

Our grade one classroom was the same as any other in the school, in almost every way. It had a high ceiling with banks of fluorescent lights, tall screenless windows on one side of the room, blackboards on two walls, and a cloakroom across the back. Its furnishings and décor consisted of an illustrated alphabet above the front blackboard: *Aa apple, Bb book, Cc cat, Dd dog, Ee egg*; an annotated number line, one through twenty, above the side board: *1 one, 2 two, 3 three, 4 four, 5 five*; a chalk ledge bearing white and colored chalk, a wooden pointer with a yellow rubber tip, and two blackboard erasers, one short and one long; bookshelves under the chalk ledge for the storage of spellers, readers, storybooks, and Bibles; a pencil sharpener bolted to the wall; a chart stand; thirty beige children's desks in five straight rows; and a heavy oak teacher's desk on which sat a blotter, two pencil cups—one for pencils, one for blue and red felt-tipped pens—tidy stacks of worksheets and workbooks, an attendance roster, a coffee mug, and a brass bell with a wooden handle. A framed photograph of Pope Paul VI, and a slightly smaller one of the Queen, hung above the front blackboard. To the left of the door was the room's only feature of architectural significance: a small arched recess in which stood a two-foot-tall statue of the Blessed Virgin Mary.

What set our classroom apart from all the others was the abundant evidence of our teacher's devotion to Saint Anthony of Padua, Patron Saint of Lost Things. Mrs. Applegate was a great believer in Saint Anthony's benevolence, and in thirty years of teaching first grade, she had amassed a sizable collection of Saint Anthony iconography. Banners, posters, prayer cards, drawings, and paintings covered two of the three panels of the side blackboard, as well as every inch of wall space. A nearly life-sized statue of Saint Anthony stood behind her desk and twenty-two smaller ones lined the windowsill. We had been warned: These plaster, ivory, papier-mâché, wax, ebony, marble, jade, glass, and plastic Saint Anthonys were to be admired, not touched. My desk was in the row nearest the windows, and a shiny ceramic Saint Anthony hovered over me while I worked.

Mrs. Applegate called on Saint Anthony throughout the day to locate lost things—and in a grade one classroom, there were plenty. "Children! Children, put down your pencils!" Mrs. Applegate would announce. "It seems that Dennis," or Randy or Allan or Christopher, depending on the day, "has lost his ruler," or workbook or lunch money or mitten. "Let's all pray to Saint Anthony." And every one of us interlaced our fingers and bowed our heads, while Mrs. Applegate called upon the intercession of Saint Anthony, "that what is lost may be found."

I always prayed extra hard when it was Dennis Hastings's pencil—or bookmark or permission slip or running shoe—that had gone missing. Dennis was a ruddy-faced boy with a perpetually runny nose, and the student most often in need of Saint Anthony's aid. I didn't know Dennis well, but he was often in trouble, and I wanted Saint Anthony to work miracles for him. Nine times out of ten—maybe more—the lost item was found, most often because thirty-one heads were bowed and someone spotted the errant button—or Field Day ribbon or pencil crayon or milk token—on the floor. Sometimes, another student would quietly pull an extra pencil—or eraser or ruler or crayon—from their desk and offer it up, claiming to have "found" it. It seemed this, too, counted as a Miracle of Saint Anthony.

Mrs. Applegate was elated each time. "Children, what was lost has been found! Say a prayer of thanks to Saint Anthony for his help!"

In a cigar box in the drawer of her desk, Mrs. Applegate kept Saint Anthony bookmarks and medals, which she distributed as rewards for perfect scores on spelling dictation or math tests. I received four bookmarks and one medal that year. I hid them in the bottom of my pencil case to keep them safe. But when I cleaned out my pencil case at the end of June, the medal was not there. My mother said this was ironic. I wasn't sure what that meant. I knew it was my own fault.

---

She arrived exactly one month after my sixth birthday. I knew I was going to have a little sister or brother, but I did not understand what that would mean, what she would be to me and I to her, even from the start. While she was pregnant, my mother had cut flannel squares to make diapers for my doll and showed me how to fold and fit them with safety pins without stabbing my thumb. I swaddled the doll tightly and tucked it into the waiting bassinet. When Rachel took the doll's place, I was awestruck. I spent hours leaning into the bassinet while she slept. Her breath was whisper-soft, and her mouth twitched as though she had something she needed to say, some urgent message just for me. I breathed in her sweet scent, slightly sour and yeasty, like fresh bread.

Her crib was in my room, and I talked to her at night through the rails. Sometimes her eyes would open and even in the darkness, I could see them glisten, inky and bottomless. She would coo and sigh, and I would tell her all the things I knew for sure: how to hold your breath and blow bubbles at swimming lessons; how to do a flip on the monkey bars; how to spell out twenty-five random words: M-O-M, D-A-D, B-A-B-Y, L-O-V-E, Y-E-S, N-O, S-U-N, F-U-N, S-N-O-W, T-R-E-E, F-L-O-W-E-R, D-O-G, C-A-T, H-A-T, F-A-T, C-A-R, H-O-T, A-P-P-L-E, R-E-D, G-R-E-E-N, B-L-U-E, J-E-S-U-S, E-X-I-T, D-A-N-G-E-R, S-T-O-P; the hiding place at the back of my closet where I kept my Halloween candy; which kids in my class were *good* and which were *bad*; how to creep down the stairs and listen without being seen. Rachel took it all in, not because she was an empty thing waiting to be filled, but because she was open wide and the world was new to her. She was unguarded in ways I could never be. Her laugh was the biggest in the room, though she was the smallest. She commanded attention. She wasn't needy or greedy about it, just more alive, more animated, more connected than most. Any rules about big sister–little sister relationships did not apply; I was a moon in her orbit.

---

On the day of Rachel's christening, I woke extra early, excited about the white sheet cake with pink sugar roses waiting in the basement fridge and the fancy dress I would wear, blue organza with a satin band at the waist. The ceremony took place after mass, and Father invited us to gather around the baptismal font: my mom and dad; my mother's Auntie Joan; her cousins Bernie and Pat, who would be Rachel's godparents; and a few neighbors. Next to the font was a wooden box, and Father motioned for me to stand on it so I could see as he poured the water on Rachel's forehead. As he said the special blessing, he asked us all to place our hands on Rachel, and my small hand was right over her heart. I beamed with pride.

After the service, my dad and Pat took turns taking photos: Rachel with her godparents, with my parents and me, then all of us with Father. As they started to move outside to take a picture on the church steps, I realized I had to pee. "Mom," I whispered, tugging at her sleeve, "I have to go."

"Oh, honey, just a minute. Bernie, can you take the baby?"

Just then, Father stepped in. "I've got this. I'll take her, you go ahead," he said, folding his hand around mine.

"Thank you, Father. If you're sure," my mother said, moving toward the door.

Father and I walked across the altar and into the sacristy, a large bright room with a high ceiling. "Here we are," Father said as we reached the bathroom. It was very small, just a toilet with a shiny black seat and a white pedestal sink. He filled the doorway, and I stood awkwardly beside the toilet. "Hop up there, now," he said, smiling. I felt a little wobbly, but I did as I was told, edging my bottom onto the cold seat, my feet dangling. Then he said, "Give me those panties."

I didn't know what to think. *Why would I take off my underwear?* I looked at the white cotton bunched around my knees. My dress crinkled as I squirmed.

"Come now," he said. "I can see those are damp. Your mother will be disappointed in you."

But I knew they weren't wet. They couldn't be. I didn't have accidents. I wasn't a baby.

Father stared, unblinking, as I eased the underwear over my frilly white ankle socks and Mary Janes. "There we go," he said. "Good girl." Then he shoved the underwear into the deep pocket of his cassock and walked away. "Hurry up now. Let's not keep them waiting."

I couldn't pee. My face burned and my head buzzed. I stood, smoothing the crinoline of my dress flat against my thighs, and flushed the toilet. I turned the cold water tap and watched the water run down the drain. "All set?" Father asked.

As I followed him back through the church, I could hear everyone outside talking. Rachel squealed and waved her arms as I approached. "Let's get going," my dad said. "I'm starved!"

In the car, the vinyl seat was sticky against my legs, and I pulled my dress over my knees. A lump grew in my throat, and I swallowed it down. Shame stained my cheeks and ears. "Are you hot, honey?" my mother asked. "Roll down your window a little." As soon as we got home, I ran upstairs and got a pair of underwear from my dresser. I balled up the dress and hid it in the back of the closet and put on my favorite jeans and Montreal Expos T-shirt. When I went downstairs, Father was sitting in the living room with Auntie Joan and the neighbors, a sweaty drink in his hand. He smiled and said, "Well, well! Where's the pretty little girl who was at church this morning?" Everyone laughed. I ran into the kitchen and wrapped my arms around my mother and buried my face in her apron.

"Where's your dress?" she asked as she peeled my arms from her middle. "For heaven's sake! You talked about that dress for weeks, now you've gone and changed the minute we're home."

I stared at my bare feet. I'd forgotten socks. A tear splashed onto my big toe.

My mother continued to lift the Saran Wrap from the trays of sandwiches and deviled eggs. "Well, come now. You're fine. Make yourself useful. We have guests." She brushed by me and pulled more food from the fridge. "Why don't you be a big girl and go offer them some punch?"

I walked into the living room and stood beside my dad, who was entertaining everyone by tossing Rachel high into the air. She giggled and cooed, and everyone clapped and laughed. I'd always felt so big, so proud when I was with Rachel. Now, I felt so small I could have slithered under the couch.

---

In grade two, my class made our First Communion. This required weeks of preparation, as we would be eating Jesus, which is something you have to be ready for. We would never be worthy, but we could be prepared. The only people truly worthy were Father and Sister, because they were *religious*, which meant they cracked the code of original sin. But even they had to follow the rules for Communion.

To learn these rules, we attended special classes in the church hall on Tuesday nights, put on by Sister and her helpers from the high school. At break time, the helpers set out fruit punch in Styrofoam cups and trays of cream-filled cookies, then they huddled into the kitchen and made fun of Sister behind her back. Either Sister was unaware they mocked her, or she ignored it and focused instead on making sure we didn't run in the hall.

Sister showed us a filmstrip called *The Eucharist*. In the filmstrip, boys in black suits and ties and girls in miniature wedding dresses kneel at the front of the church, and a priest places tiny white Communion wafers on their tongues. The priest looks like Father but with a brush cut and horn-rimmed glasses. You can tell the children are worthy because they close their eyes as the priest comes to give them their wafers, and the priest smiles. And you can see, even in the filmstrip, that their thoughts are pure. "When you receive the wafer, the Holy Eucharist, your thoughts must be pure," Sister told us. Holding on to pure thoughts is a feat of spiritual gymnastics. The only human with entirely pure thoughts was the Virgin Mary, who was born that way because of the Immaculate Conception. This, we learned in class, was the way God made Mary without sin. The rest of us, for thousands of years, have come up short—even Father and Sister, until they married God. Sister gave us bookmarks depicting the Assumption, a glowing Mary floating up to heaven, flying like Wonder Woman in her invisible plane.

The soundtrack for the filmstrip was on a cassette tape, which made a *ping* when it was time to advance to the next image. Sister paused the tape so many times that we ended up watching the filmstrip for three weeks. The filmstrip required a lot of additional explanation so that we might fully understand the gravity of the situation. "Children," Sister said as we stared at an image of Jesus, whose heart was simultaneously bleeding and radiating beams of light. "Look at the Sacred Heart of Jesus. Jesus' blood is pouring out for all sinners. Jesus died for your sins, but his body and blood live on in the bread and wine of the Eucharist. When we make our Holy Communion and receive his body, we must remember His sacrifice." Sister kept the hemorrhaging Jesus on the screen for a long time so we could consider this. I was mesmerized by the blood, but also confused about how one Jesus was turned into enough wine and wafers for every person in every Church in the world. When Sister asked if there were any questions, I didn't ask because I knew it was a Mystery and therefore, should not be questioned.

Sister also explained the dress code for First Communion Day. "The boys and girls in the filmstrip are wearing beautiful clothes," Sister said, but the filmstrip was made a long time ago, and we did not need to wear dark suits and white dresses. "Reform," said Sister, "has come to the Church." This meant that, in 1973, God was okay with short-sleeved shirts and pants for the boys, as long as they were clean and pressed, and nice dresses for the girls, as long as they were not sleeveless, or too short, or too colorful. "Don't draw attention," Sister told the girls. "God sees you. That's what matters." Still, when First Communion Day arrived, Sister beamed at the few girls who dressed like miniature brides in white dresses and veils. They were Immaculate, worthy of Jesus.

The final week of First Communion class, we did a practice run. Sister told us that the wafers we used for practice were not consecrated, which meant Father had not said the prayers that turned them into Jesus' body. "Still," Sister warned us, "these are holy wafers." We were to be silent and stand in a line and keep our hands to ourselves. We moved forward, one step at a time, until we reached the front of the line and closed our eyes and stuck out our tongues. Sister assessed them. "Too far," she said, or "A little more," until we presented just the right amount of Jesus-worthy tongue on which to set the wafer. The wafers tasted like white glue, not at all like Wonder Bread, which is what you would expect. We were warned: "Do not bite the wafer! This is the body of Jesus, not a cracker," so we had to let it dissolve. Chewing was forbidden. However, when I retracted the wafer, it adhered to the roof of my mouth, and, though I tried and tried, there was no way to pry it off with my tongue. Later in bed, after I had brushed my teeth, I used my fingernail to scrape the last of it away.

---

Our school was next to the church, and Father came to our classroom every Friday after lunch. From the window, we could see him leaving the rectory, a gray stone building that smelled of books and aftershave. Few people entered beyond its front office. The teacher sometimes chose two students to go deliver pennies from the penny drive or consent forms for sacrament preparation classes. Sister always answered the door. She didn't ever look happy, but she didn't look sad either. She just looked bothered, as though her veil might be a little scratchy and answering the door was not her job. "Is there anything else?" she asked each time. I was never sure what else there might be, but she always waited for an answer. "Don't dawdle on your way back to class!" she warned.

One Friday, Father came in during the math lesson, and the teacher set her chalk on the ledge and smoothed her skirt. "Children, look who's here!" Father was tall and lean, and his hair was shiny and perfect, like a Ken doll. The creases in his black shirt and black pants looked sharp enough to cut. "What do we say to Father?"

"Good afternooooon, Father!" The class waited while Father leaned in and spoke to the teacher and the teacher blushed. We waited to hear how many children Father needed to help at the rectory that day. This was an honor reserved for the chosen.

Father smiled at the class. *Pick me,* I thought and sat up straighter. *Don't see me,* I thought and closed my eyes tight. My palms were sweaty, my skin so tight and dry I could have crumbled and blown away. My stomach rumbled even though I had just eaten lunch. Some students looked out the window and watched the grade fives playing dodgeball on the playground, but I stared straight ahead and held my breath.

Father raised his arm and pointed. He picked them like ripe fruit. "One. Two. Three. Three will do." One beamed. Two reddened. Three glanced around, desperately hoping Father had pointed to the child in the next desk. One, Two, and Three filed out.

I was disappointed and relieved at the same time. I exhaled and felt perspiration form on my neck and back. I leaned forward and rested my forehead on the cool desk.

"Children!" the teacher called. "What do we say to Father?"

I sat up straight and joined the singsong reply, "Thaaaank you, Faaaather."

Father set a stack of holy cards on the teacher's desk. He smiled and blessed the class, his arm cutting like a scythe across the room.

---

We usually saw Father just twice a week—on the altar each Sunday and on Friday, when he visited the school—yet he wielded great influence on our lives. Our teachers and parents referred to him often, usually to remind us how to be good. *What did Father say in his homily last Sunday? What would Father think? Maybe we should ask Father about that....*

My mother felt that Father needed a home-cooked meal now and again, even though Sister cooked for him every day. "I wonder how Father is getting along. Maybe we should invite him for dinner."

My dad complained about Father's visits. "Geez, wasn't he just here?" he would say. "I suppose I'll have to bring out the good scotch."

"The Morans and the Donnellys have him once a month," my mother would remind him.

Being in Father's presence was a lesson in humility. Priests were chosen for a higher calling, and everybody else was much, much lower by comparison. Once a year, during Vocation Week, our class said special prayers to convince God to call more people to become priests and nuns. God could call anyone; the decision was His alone. God could choose any of us at any time, whether we wanted to be chosen or not. You never knew when God would call, so you had to be ready. During Vocation Week, we also prayed for the young men in the seminary studying to become priests. One year, we were each given a tiny slip of paper with the name of a seminarian. *Pray for* Robert. *Pray for* James. *Pray for* Martin. We were to pray for our seminarian each night before bed. We were to fall asleep asking God to make those who were already good enough into superheroes of goodness. The Church needed more priests. There were never enough.

When Father came for dinner, we ate in the dining room. Mother used the special blue-and-white china and served roast beef with cake for dessert even though Father insisted we not make a fuss. Rachel and I wore our church clothes all afternoon, and I tried not to get my dress dirty before dinner. We all bowed our heads when Father said grace and pretended this was something we did every day. We laughed at Father's jokes. I used my best manners. I sat up straight and didn't spit the gristly pieces of meat onto my plate or feed bits to the dog under the table. I asked, *May I please be excused?* and went to bed without complaining.

Sometimes Father came upstairs to tuck us in. *Aren't we lucky?* I thought as I climbed between the cool, crisp sheets. Father smiled and told us we were Special Girls. He lifted Rachel into her bed and raised her bed rail. Then, he sat on the edge of my bed. He made a cross on my forehead and said a prayer. He asked Jesus to help us always listen to our parents and teachers and do as we are told. "Close your eyes," he said. His hands tucked the bedding around me, against my shoulders, along my sides, down my legs. I wanted to say, *Too tight, too tight! No....* But I couldn't breathe. He leaned on me, the weight of him crushing my ribcage. *Good night, Sweetheart*, he said. He kissed me on my mouth, his lips wet and hot, his whiskers prickly as nettles.

I couldn't fall asleep. I could hear my parents and Father chatting, their easy conversation and laughter drifting up the stairs. I rubbed my face on the sheet, but the scent of his cologne was deep in my skin. I kept my eyes closed tight and tried to remember how lucky I was to be chosen, to be Father's Special Girl, but all I could think was *Too tight, too tight. No no no no no.*

Hours later, Father left, and my parents came up to bed. My mother leaned into the room to check on me and Rachel, and I pretended to be asleep. I knew my mother would be smiling, satisfied that we were *snug as a bug in a rug*. Safe as houses.

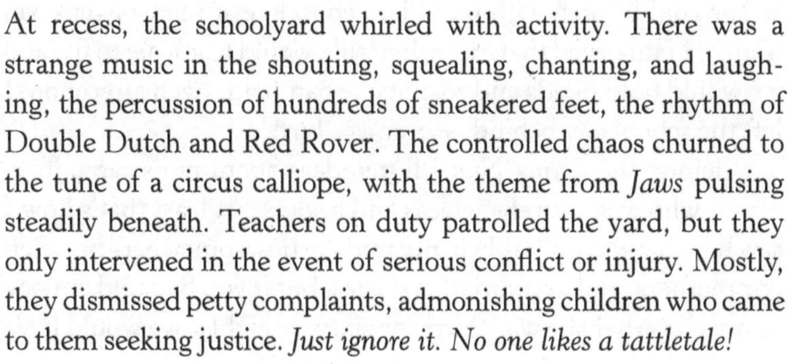

At recess, the schoolyard whirled with activity. There was a strange music in the shouting, squealing, chanting, and laughing, the percussion of hundreds of sneakered feet, the rhythm of Double Dutch and Red Rover. The controlled chaos churned to the tune of a circus calliope, with the theme from *Jaws* pulsing steadily beneath. Teachers on duty patrolled the yard, but they only intervened in the event of serious conflict or injury. Mostly, they dismissed petty complaints, admonishing children who came to them seeking justice. *Just ignore it. No one likes a tattletale!*

When Father visited the schoolyard, the younger children swarmed him, vying to hold his hand or receive a butterscotch candy from his jacket pocket. His grandfatherly kindness was irresistible. He smiled as he ruffled hair and pinched cheeks, but he never stood still. Weaving through skipping ropes and dodgeball matches, he made his way across the vast blacktop like a shark, meandering and patient but sharply alert. He changed course unexpectedly, stopping briefly to embrace one child then quickly moving on to stroke the shoulders of another.

In science class we learned that a shark can smell the tiniest drop of blood in seawater—as little as one part per million. The slightest weakness, a benign flaw, would alert the shark to unsuspecting prey. They didn't stand a chance.

---

I raced home every day after school to watch my favorite TV shows: *The Partridge Family*, *The Brady Bunch*, and my very favorite, *The Flying Nun*. Just before five o'clock, I put on my cream-colored poncho and a white coronet, just like Sister Bertrille's, which I had folded from four pieces of cardboard from Mother's pantyhose packages. I made a smaller one for Rachel so she could watch with me. I longed to live at the Convent San Tanco. I fantasized that Sister Bertrille would teach me to fly, and we would hold hands and soar above San Juan. Each afternoon, I left the school day behind, as free as a bird.

Before *The Flying Nun*, all my ideas about nuns came from Sister, who was entirely ageless and sexless. At least that's how I saw her. She was probably in her mid-forties, somewhere between our mothers' and grandmothers' ages, but if you had told anyone in my class that she was thirty, or sixty, or eighty, we would have believed it. She wore a light blue habit—a shapeless dress that came just below her knees—and a starched, white veil, bobby-pinned in place to expose precisely one inch of her hairline. Her dress had deep pockets in which she kept a rosary, Kleenex, chalk, and a sizable collection of holy cards to give to deserving children. Sister was intimidating, and no one, not even the perfect girls, wanted to be the sole focus of her attention. Even our teacher was ruffled by Sister's visits. When Father arrived, the teacher smiled and blushed, happily nervous in his presence. But when Sister came to the door, the teacher became quiet and serious, and that was our cue to do the same.

The September I started grade three, a new nun arrived in the parish. Sister Sharron was young—much younger than Sister. Her hair was cut in a trendy shag like Mrs. Partridge, and she wore regular clothes. She was tiny, not much taller than me, and her high-pitched laugh bounced down the hallway. Our very own Sister Bertrille.

At first, Sister and Sister Sharron came together for class visits. Sister told us that Sister Sharron was still a nun-in-training—*a novice*, Sister called her—because she had not yet *taken final vows.* Sister explained that these vows were how nuns married Jesus, and Sister Sharron was still *in discernment.* So, until she decided whether or not to take Jesus up on his proposal, Sister Sharron followed Sister around. When Sister was watching, Sister Sharron was subdued, but when Sister left the room, Sister Sharron's face opened into a wide smile. After several weeks, Sister Sharron began coming by herself for class visits. She brought a worn acoustic guitar with a wide macramé strap and sang Cat Stevens, Bob Dylan, and Peter, Paul and Mary songs. I adored her. I think we all did. During her visits, I sat tall in my desk and took care to follow along with the lyrics on the chart paper, so as not to make even a tiny mistake. One week, she picked me to stand beside her and turn the pages of her songbook, and my heart felt like it might burst. I was so proud to be chosen.

Another week, Sister Sharron visited at the end of the day, and after our sing-along, she lined us up for dismissal. I hurried in the cloakroom so I could be at the front of the line. As we waited for everyone to line up, Sister Sharron rested her hand on my shoulder. "You have a lovely voice," she said. "You should come to Children's Choir on Saturdays." I couldn't speak. *She heard me,* I thought. *She heard me.*

---

One evening, as I sat at the dining room table with my math homework, I heard my parents talking about Sister.

Scouring the roasting pan with an SOS pad, my mother said, "Jean phoned this afternoon. She was telling me that Sister got into some trouble at the school. Jean's the head of the PTA, so she would know. That little Hastings boy, the one with the freckles, I guess he was acting up in class during Sister's visit, and she hauled him out of his desk and dragged him down to the office. She dislocated his shoulder. Can you imagine? That poor child!"

"Well," my dad replied from behind his newspaper, "I wouldn't be so sure that was all Sister's doing. If he tried to run away from her, he probably pulled it out of joint himself."

"How can you blame a little boy for such a serious injury? She's an adult! She should know better."

"You don't know that boy. He might be a little bugger. You've gotta be firm with kids like that. It's the only way to keep them in line."

My mother turned her back and began drying the dishes.

"His shoulder probably popped right back into the socket. Like I said, he probably brought it on himself, one way or another. Sister knows kids. She uses a firm hand, and that's not a bad thing."

"Now how would Sister know anything about children?" Mom said.

"Sister's been in schools for years. Those nuns who taught when I was a kid were sure tough on us, and look how well I turned out," Dad said, chuckling.

My mother smiled and shook her head. "I'm just saying, Sister should have been more careful. That poor boy."

That night I lay in bed, confused by my parents' conversation. I had only ever heard them say nice things about Sister—how she was *devoted to the school* and *works so hard*. It was unsettling to know they saw the other side of her, the side that had always made me nervous. I wasn't surprised about what happened. Dennis Hastings had been in my class in grade one, and I knew he was the sort of boy Sister did not tolerate. She was kind to the good girls, the ones she praised for their perfect manners, hygiene, and piety, and to the few boys who were passably clean and sat still during her visits. But with those who did not meet her expectations, Sister was harsh. *For your own good*, she would say as she yanked an ear or pulled a braid to get a child's attention. I was somewhere in the middle—sometimes good, but sometimes not—so I got a taste of both Sisters, the sweet and the sour.

The next morning, reports of Dennis's run-in with Sister swirled around the schoolyard. I stood alone in the center of the yard, my spine against the flagpole and my eyes shut tight, and gathered them in like crisp autumn leaves.

*It happened during rosary. He was playing with a matchbox car, and she told him to give it to her and he wouldn't. She had to pry it out of his hand.... Dennis is always in trouble.... Sister told him to kneel in the corner.... He said something Sister couldn't hear, and everybody laughed.... She yanked him out of his desk.... She did that to my sister once.... He deserved it.... You could hear them going down the hall, the way her shoes click when she's mad.... Sister Sharron was in our class. She went into the hall to see what was going on.... They were in Mr. Mackenzie's office for an hour.... More like two hours....*

*Dennis's dad came after school.... I saw them leave. Dennis's face was bright red.... His brother told me he had to go to the hospital.... His arm is in a sling.... My mom said Sister went too far.*

As quickly as the story came together, it disappeared, taken away on the wind. In a few days, Dennis no longer wore the sling, and we all went on as though nothing had ever happened.

That same week, Sister Sharron left. I couldn't be sure—I had no proof—but I wondered if her leaving had something to do with the Dennis Hastings incident, something to do with Sister. Maybe Sister Sharron saw what really happened, or maybe she hadn't taken Sister's side. Whatever the case, Sister Sharron left without saying goodbye, without explanation. For weeks I watched for her in the halls, holding on to the thin hope that she would return. I wondered if she thought of us, of me, if she knew how desperately I wanted her to come back.

When Sister resumed her visits to our class, instead of sing-alongs, we prayed the rosary. I felt such bitterness I could hardly look at Sister. I wanted her to notice my anger and resentment, wanted her to know how much I disliked her. Instead, she took my lowered head as a sign of piety. "Good girl," she said as she walked between the rows of desks. "The Blessed Virgin loves girls who bow their heads and lower their eyes. Obedience is a virtue." A great roar of anger filled my ears. I tightened my grip on my rosary and dug the crucifix under my thumbnail until it bled and my rage subsided.

During Community Helpers week, the entire school sat on the floor of the gym for a presentation on Stranger Danger. The visiting police officer looked like he had stepped out of our social studies book—tall and broad-shouldered in his crisp blue uniform, the brim of his cap gleaming under the fluorescent lights of the gym. "Good afternoon, boys and girls," he began. "I'm here today to discuss a matter of grave importance." The lights dimmed and words appeared on the portable screen behind him: STRANGER DANGER: WHAT YOU NEED TO KNOW. The officer narrated a series of slides, describing how each showed potential Stranger Danger. A man in dark clothing standing behind a tree in a playground. A girl walking past a shadowy alley at night. A man in a car with the window rolled down, a map in his hand, asking two children for directions.

I watched, wide-eyed and nodding—we all did. The man in the slides looked ordinary enough, but, the officer warned, he was a *predator* who would *take advantage* of children like us. Because the officer did not describe this *taking advantage* in detail, I knew it must be especially bad.

Then the officer went through a list of rules we should follow to minimize Stranger Danger. *Don't talk to strangers. Don't go out after dark. Don't walk home alone. Don't get into a car with someone you don't know. If you see a suspicious man, tell a trusted adult....* The list was meant to be reassuring. "If you just follow these simple rules," the officer promised, the corners of his mouth curled in a tight smile, "you'll be safe."

What he didn't say, what he didn't seem to know, was that following the rules was no guarantee. That you could know every rule and follow them to a tee, and still, danger lurked in the most unexpected places. That the schoolyard and the church hall were as dangerous as a dark alley. That the everydayness of things tricked you into letting your guard down. I knew with absolute certainty that familiar people and places posed a more sinister threat than the unknown or unknowable. The man in the slides was a master of disguise. Even if you were able spot the stranger or the danger, where would you find the trusted adult you were supposed to tell? Trust was a slippery thing: You might have a grip on it one minute and lose it the next.

In fourth grade, we made our First Confession. *The Sacrament of Reconciliation,* Sister called it. *An invitation to repentance and forgiveness.* For six weeks before First Confession, Sister visited our classroom. Mostly, she talked about *original sin.* Everyone, except the Virgin Mary and Jesus who are pure and not sinful like the rest of us, was born with what Sister called *the stain of original sin.* Original sin is a stain that can never be fully washed out but that might be managed by being a good Catholic and going to confession often. I pictured a blood stain on a white T-shirt. My mother scrubbed such stains with salt and a toothbrush, or with Sunlight soap that smelled of lemons and metal, but the stains never fully lifted. Original sin is like that: It can fade, but it is never fully removed. We go to confession anyway, to keep the stain as light as possible.

We practiced, with Sister playing the role of priest. We were to memorize the script: *Bless me, Father, for I have sinned*...and then name three sins. Sister said to choose just three because Father didn't have all day. "Choose the most serious transgressions," Sister told us. All our other wrongdoings would be forgiven too, according to Sister. She taught us to end our confession with, *For these and all my sins I am truly sorry*—a disclaimer to cover all our offenses.

I considered what my three most serious transgressions might be. Sister had us write these sins on index cards so we wouldn't forget. *I lied to my mother. I stole penny candy from the counter at the corner store. I had impure thoughts.* I wasn't sure what impure thoughts were specifically, but according to Sister we all have them. I knew these were sins of the body because the thoughts were inside us, in our heads and our hearts, so it was essential they be revealed and atoned for.

Sister explained that we needed to be completely honest when we confessed our sins. "Priests are bound by the Seal of the Confessional," Sister told us. "What you say to the priest in confession, he can never tell a soul." I tried to imagine it: thousands and thousands of secrets—maybe millions—all inside Father, sealed there for eternity. Of course, it would be a big job carrying all those sins around. He knew the worst things everyone had ever done and could see deep inside us, inside our weak, pitiful hearts. It was like being a mind reader, I figured—not the first superpower most people would choose but still a wonderful, terrible power.

One afternoon, Sister walked us to the church to see the confessional, the tiny closet where we would make our confession. She pulled back the heavy velvet curtain, and the confessional smelled of dry wood and something unidentifiable. Fear, perhaps. Or hopelessness. Sister showed us how when a person knelt on the kneeler, a little light went on above the confessional to indicate it was occupied. It flashed on, off, on, off, on, off, like a fridge light. Then she let us take turns kneeling in the confessional, so we would know what to expect. When it was my turn, I knelt and then squinted and tried to see through the screen that would separate me from Father. Sister demonstrated how the screen slid open and closed but told us not to touch it, that it could only be opened from Father's side. If Father wanted to, he would open the screen and speak to us face-to-face. But we were to stay on script, Sister warned, to use only the words we'd practiced and the three sins we had memorized, and to answer Father only if he asked a question. Late at night, I wondered what Father might ask. What could he want to know? Sister said he would also give us a special blessing—an Absolution—and assign our penance, probably ten Hail Marys so the Blessed Virgin would help us be better in the future. We were to return to our pews and do our penance immediately.

On the day of First Confession, I did exactly as Sister said. I sat quietly in the pew and prayed, then we all lined up at the confessional, and I waited my turn. *Bless me, Father*, I began. I could not see Father, but I could hear his waxy voice behind the screen and smell his aftershave. He assigned my penance: five Hail Marys. With my head bowed, I could see the shadow of his hand passing over, and I flinched, just slightly. *In the name of the Father, and of the Son....* In a blurred moment, it was over, and I bolted from the confessional. I returned to my seat, perched on the kneeler to pray, and pressed my sweaty palms together. My skin prickled, the way it always did after I had been near Father, and I couldn't concentrate on my Hail Marys. I tried to think about how confession had washed away all my past sins. I wondered how long the sinlessness would last, how long I could remain pure like the Blessed Virgin.

That night, lying in bed, I began to think about the stain of sin bleeding through me, rising to the surface and seeping out through my pores. Sometimes, it was bloodred, and other times, it was as black as pitch. I pictured freshly tarred roads and bottomless tarpits with steam rising from their surfaces. I squeezed my eyes shut, trying to regain the feeling of cleanliness after confession, but it was gone. Maybe it was never there after all.

---

It had been rumored for years, but no one saw it coming. *It's about time*, some people said. *There's no need for it*, said others. *It's not that big a deal*, said a few. But it was a big deal, at least to the girls I knew.

When my mother read about the meeting in the bulletin, she said, "I never thought I'd see the day! But now that it's here, I think you should go. I mean, if you want to." I didn't want to, but that Monday at school it was all the girls talked about.

During her weekly visit, Sister spoke about it to the class. "After much prayer and discernment, our Bishop has determined it is appropriate to introduce female altar servers. This is being done on a strictly experimental basis. The traditions and laws of the Church have restricted this ministry to boys and men. And yet, as the Church changes with the times, so should Her interpretations of the law. Some of you girls will want to consider this very important ministry." She sounded so formal, even for Sister. I couldn't tell if she was gratified or annoyed. That was always the way with Sister. The girls sat taller in their desks and ignored the smug snorts of the boys who would soon be forced to share their special status.

That night at dinner, I asked my mother if she would drive me to the altar girls' meeting on Saturday. I could tell she was pleased. "That's a good decision," she said. "A *very* good decision. You're almost eleven. It's time you started to get involved at the church. I know you go to the rectory with Father to help fold bulletins, but this is different. It's an honor to serve on the altar."

I wanted to go to the meeting, if only to please my mother. But her mention of the afternoons at the rectory with Father made my stomach hurt. "May I be excused?" I asked.

"No dessert? I made butterscotch pudding, your favorite."

I forced a smile and left the table. As I climbed the stairs, I heard Rachel say, "I'll have my pudding and hers!" and the three of them laughed and teased as they cleared the dinner plates.

I went to my room and laid out my clothes for the next day, then ran my bath. I added three capfuls of bubble bath so that when I laid back in the tub, my body was covered in mounds of bubbles. I held my breath, then slid down until I was flat on my back. I stayed under for as long as I could, then sat up and gulped for air. I did it again and again, until I was lightheaded. My thoughts were waterlogged, and the horrible memories of the afternoons at the rectory with Father became murky and dull. By the time my mother came upstairs and called to me to hurry so she could give Rachel her bath, I was shivering in the tepid water.

On Saturday afternoon, thirteen girls, me among them, gathered in the church for an orientation session led by Deacon Ted, the priest-in-training assigned to our parish. Deacon Ted looked like a six-and-a-half-foot-tall twelve-year-old, all limbs and neck, arms waving and Adam's apple bobbing as he spoke. He explained that one of his duties was to be the parish sacristan, which meant he was in charge of all the preparations for mass: the altar linens and candles, the chalice and patens, the wafers and wine. After passing around an attendance sheet, he took us onto the altar and walked us slowly through the parts of the mass, explaining the altar servers' duties step by step: how to walk in the procession, when to sit, when to stand, how to light and snuff the candles, where to place the chalice on the altar, how to pour water on Father's fingertips and offer him the starched white cloth, when to ring the tiny gold bell. We had all been to mass thousands of times, but these details seemed suddenly new and important. "Remember," he told us, "you will be serving Father. When he celebrates the Eucharist, Father is Christ Among Us. It is an honor to serve on the altar and assist Father. You will perform all the tasks I have shown you and more. Anything Father asks." I felt a surge of panic. I glanced at the girls to the left and right of me who were nodding, reverent and sincere. I nodded too. Everyone knew I was one of Father's Special Helpers. I didn't want them to know anything more than that. I stared straight ahead and bit the inside of my cheek until it bled.

Then, Deacon Ted led us into the sacristy and showed us the credence, a special dresser with more than a dozen shallow drawers for Father's vestments. He opened each drawer and ran his hands over the heavy silk stoles and chasubles in purple, green, and red. The altar servers' hooded robes were stored in a tall armoire, hanging like skinny boys from shortest to tallest. "Your robe must come to your ankles, not below and not above. You will wear dark pants and black shoes, no sandals. And girls, you are not to wear earrings or makeup. No bows in your hair. This is mass, not a fashion show." As he said this, Deacon Ted looked cross, but then he burst into a wide smile. "Ah, but I know we'll have no trouble with you girls. You'll be all that the boys are and better. Good little helpers, every one of you."

The final event of the day was a pizza party in the church hall. As Deacon Ted herded us toward the back exit of the sacristy, the girls ahead of me burst into nervous giggles. I hung back and peered into the tiny bathroom. The sight of the toilet made me queasy. I glanced up and saw Deacon Ted's reflection behind me in the mirror. "Are you okay, Sweetheart?" he asked. I fell to my knees and heaved into the bleach-white bowl.

---

For weeks after the altar servers' meeting, foggy memories descended like shadows and spread over me like prickly heat, often in the night, but sometimes in the daytime too.

*I shed my slicker and place my rain boots on the mat. I know the room with its dark wood panelling and leather furniture. It smells of aftershave and Binaca, and I taste a bitter dread rising in my throat. Black cuffs, leather watchband, fine brown hairs on the back of a hand. Sitting on the arm of a sofa or held too tightly on a lap. A warm hand on my back, my neck, my stomach, my thighs. Bruising pressure between my legs, then a sharp sting. Tree branches outside a high window whipping in the wind, tap-tap-tapping on the pane.*

These images moved in and out of focus, sometimes wrenching me from nightmares or daydreams and jarring me awake.

Because these real-but-not-real moments were unpredictable, I was always vigilant. At night, I stayed awake as late as I could, until my eyes were lead-heavy with sleep. In the daytime, the knowing-but-not-knowing made me feel quiet and small. It stripped me naked, and though I wore undershirts and turtlenecks and wool cardigans, I was cold all the time.

---

I was an altar server for a few weeks, then I asked Deacon Ted to take me off the schedule. "It's not for me," I told him. "I don't feel ready." When my mother asked why I wasn't serving anymore, I lied. "They had too many. They needed a few of us to drop out." I felt guilty for lying to her, but also relieved. The few times I'd served as an altar-girl-in-training, my hands shook so much I thought I might spill the wine. I knew Father couldn't hurt me on the altar, but just being near him made me nervous.

My mother was insistent that I take on a new extracurricular activity. "You need to get involved," she said again and again, as we sat in the car waiting for Rachel to emerge from swimming lessons, and ballet, and piano, and tae kwon do. "I'm sure you're good at any number of things. You just need to try. What about softball? An art class? Youth choir?" I stayed silent and waited for these moments to pass. But she kept prodding, and eventually, I had to choose an activity. Though three years had passed, I had not forgotten what Sister Sharron had said: *You have a lovely voice*. Her praise should have given me confidence and made me want to sing, but it had had the opposite effect: It made me want to keep her compliment all to myself, as though acting on it would dilute its power. But finally, to pacify my mother, I joined the choir.

Youth choir practices were held in the cathedral on Thursday evenings. I'd never been in the choir loft, and I scurried as quickly as possible up the winding steps. The narrow passage, lit by only two dim bulbs, one at the bottom and one at the top, was just wide enough for one person. From light to dark to light took maybe fifteen seconds, but it seemed like forever. I didn't dare think what I would do if I became trapped.

Although I dreaded the sinister staircase, it turned out to be worth the climb. The air in the vault of the cathedral was warm and soft, and I felt safe suspended high above the pews. It was as though time was suspended too, and I didn't have to think about anything but the music. When I was singing, I didn't have to figure out what to say, how much to reveal, and when. I'd always been quiet. *Painfully shy,* I once heard a teacher whisper to my mother. It wasn't usually painful, though. Mostly, I wore quiet like a woollen shawl, protective and comforting. And singing offered a controlled release of all I didn't say, all I held in—a way to let off just enough but not too much steam—like a relief valve on an old-fashioned pressure cooker.

At twelve, I was the youngest choir member. I was intimidated by the talent and confidence of the others, but also curious about who they were and what brought them there. I had a sense, even from the first day, that the other choir members were people like me, people who didn't usually fit in. People no one sat with on the bus, at least not by choice. People who wore plaid pants and oversized blazers or Wrangler jeans and nubbly grandma-knit scarves. Faces I'd seen at the library and the swimming pool but had looked past or through. But when they sang, it was wondrous. The convergence of voices, the confluence of pitch and tone and subtle inflection, was blessed and holy. All the years I'd sat in a pew listening, the thousands of times I'd genuflected, knelt, daydreamed, and shuffled toward the altar for Communion, I had never heard a choir the way I did standing among them, singing in harmony with them.

My mother's Catholic Women's League meetings were also on Thursday nights at seven, and we usually finished at the same time, at nine. However, in early December, the CWL held their Christmas social, which was at a member's home rather than the parish hall. My mother decided she would drop me off at practice, then leave the party early to come back and pick me up again at nine.

When she pulled into the parking lot of the cathedral to drop me off, Father was on his way out. He waved, and my mother rolled down her window, and he stopped to talk.

"You must come by for a drink during the holidays, Father," my mother insisted.

"Oh, yes, yes, I'd love to." Father leaned into the car. "And I'll bet you're here for choir practice."

"Yes, Father," I said, unbuckling my seatbelt and opening the door.

"You know," Father said to my mother, "if you're off to the CWL Christmas party, I can run her home for you. It's no trouble. No trouble at all."

"No! I can get a ride!" I said quickly.

My mother gave me her mind-your-manners-Young-Lady look, then turned to Father. "That's so kind of you, Father. I haven't had a night out with the girls in so long. I think I'll take you up on that offer."

"Okay, then," Father said, grinning at me. "I'll see you at nine."

I ran inside, and when I reached the choir loft, I was out of breath. I dropped my folder of Christmas music, and the pages fluttered to the floor. I gathered them as the choir director led warm-ups. We were rehearsing carols for Midnight Mass. The youth choir was to lead carolling from ten until eleven, then the adult choir would sing for the service. We rehearsed a few of the easier songs—"Joy to the World" and "Away in a Manger"—then we came to "The Huron Carol." The director had given me a solo, and I had practiced all week. But I was so distracted about Father driving me home that I couldn't get my entry right.

"Okay, stop. Let's try that again," the choir director said.

*Focus*, I thought. *Focus.* My solo was at the beginning of the fourth verse. The choir sang the first verse, then the second. *Focus, focus.... You can do this. It will all be okay. He will drive me home, that's all. I'll put my seatbelt on. He'll make small talk. He'll say all the usual things, ask about school, call me his special girl.... He will take my hand, and I'll just let him. I won't make a big deal about it. If he reaches for my leg, I'll move over. It's a five-minute drive.... But he always squeezes my hand too tight, puts my hand on his thigh, says "good girl, good girl," pushes my hand between his legs, massages my shoulder, slips his hand inside my sweater.... I'll just close my eyes. It's a five-minute drive....*

"Stop, stop," the choir director said, trying to hide his impatience. I had missed my entrance again. "You have to watch. I'll cue you and count you in. Just like last week. Remember?"

After three tries, I finally came in on the right beat. My throat was tight, and I missed a couple of notes. I could have crawled under a pew.

"That was not bad," the choir director said. "We still have a few weeks to work on it. Keep practicing. Okay, everybody. Let's take ten."

I began putting my sheet music in order while everyone else sat around talking. And then it came to me: I could ask Stephanie for a ride home. I didn't know her very well—she was at least seventeen, maybe eighteen—but she lived on my block, so it would be easy for her to drive me, and I could make up an excuse for Father.

Stephanie was sitting with a group of older kids, laughing loudly and polishing her flute with a scrap of flannel. I walked over to them and said, "Um, Stephanie. Hi. I was wondering, could I get a ride home with you?"

"Yeah, sure, I can drop you off," she replied. "I think I go right past your house."

"Thanks," I said. Stephanie smiled and turned back to her friends.

I was anxious about making an excuse to Father, but relieved too. I was a little more focused through the second half of practice. When we were dismissed, I was gathering up my music when Stephanie said, "I'll see you downstairs. No rush."

By the time I reached the foyer, Stephanie was talking to Father. "...but really, Father, I'm happy to drop her off. She lives right on my street."

"Well, I promised her mother—"

"It's okay, really. Our moms are both at the CWL. Her mother will be absolutely fine with me dropping her off. Oh, here she is now." Stephanie turned to me. "Let's go!" She grabbed my coat sleeve and pulled me toward the door. "Bye, Father!" she called without looking back.

I turned and said, "Thank you anyway, Father," and we hurried out into the cold night.

Stephanie set the heat on high, and we shivered as we waited for the car to warm up. "That was a close one," she said. "I sure wouldn't want to get in a car with Father Feeler."

I turned toward her, my eyes wide.

She spoke so quickly I could hardly keep up. "You know about Father Feeler, right? I mean, that's what *everybody* calls him. He's sooooo creepy. Always trying to cop a feel. I remember when I was in grade school, he hung around the monkey bars trying to look up the girls' skirts. Good old Father Feeler! He's such a freak. And, like, everybody knows about him, but nobody says anything. It's bizarre. Anyway, anytime you need a ride, just ask." She turned on the radio and popped a cassette in the tape deck. "Do you like Heart? You know, the band? They're the coolest! Listen to this." She fast-forwarded the tape to "Dreamboat Annie" and turned up the volume. She sang along, tapping her hands on the steering wheel.

When she pulled up in front of my house, she turned down the volume a little. "Hey, what I said about Father—don't let it bother you. I mean, he's creepy, but you just have to watch out, you know? And once you get to high school, he's never around. Spends all his time with the little kids. I mean, not that you're a little kid. You're in, what, sixth grade?"

"Yeah," I said. "Thanks again for the ride."

As I stood on the sidewalk and watched Stephanie drive away, I considered all the things she said and all the things she didn't. *You just have to watch out.* Did she hear this from the girls in her class, or maybe an older cousin? Or did she just *know* somehow? Was she onto Father from the start, and then had the agility to avoid being caught? In English class, we were studying idioms. *A wolf in sheep's clothing. That's Father*, I thought. Only some girls saw the disguise, and some met the wolf.

---

By eighth grade, all the popular girls played basketball. In September, whether we showed any interest or not, we were marshalled to the gym for tryouts. I didn't want to go, but I couldn't imagine the scrutiny that would come with being left out. Making the team meant there might be some hope for you in high school, that you had at least a chance of being, if not popular, then seen. I made the team. Four afternoons a week, we donned our practice jerseys, ran laps around the gym, practiced free throws, and played half-court games. We moved like spring colts, awkward on our too-long legs.

One afternoon at the beginning of practice, Coach blew his whistle and yelled, "Huddle up!" We all ran to center court. "We have a new assistant coach," he said. "Father is going to help me out this year. He played varsity ball in college, so he knows his stuff." And there he was in the doorway of the gym: Father in wind pants and a rugby shirt, a basketball under his arm. Even without his Roman collar, he looked like a priest. He smiled and raised his hand in a smooth hybrid gesture of wave and blessing. Beside Father stood a girl with shiny dark hair. I didn't know her name, but she went to our school. She was younger than me and older than Rachel. I'd noticed her in the halls. She had Rachel's haircut, the same lithe body and open smile. "And that's Jenna," Coach said. "She may be younger, but she can outplay most of you. She's the best player the junior team's ever had. I've asked her to practice with us. She'll keep you on your toes." Jenna smiled up at Father, and he put his hand on the back of her neck. A chill gripped me between my shoulder blades.

Coach blew two short whistles, the signal to line up for drills. But I didn't move. I stared at Father as though he were an apparition. Coach passed behind me and swatted me on the bottom with his clipboard. "Gonna join us or what, kiddo?" I followed the other girls, but I couldn't feel my feet or my hands, couldn't judge the distance to the net. "C'mon! C'mon, girls! Show Father what you can do!" Coach whistled again and we stopped, a lone ball bouncing into the corner of the gym.

"Looking good, girls," Father said. "Now let's work on those layups." We lined up in front of the net, and Father demonstrated.

"Right, left, *up*!" The ball dropped from his palm into the net. "Come on up here, Jenna. Let's show them how it's done." We watched as Father guided Jenna through a layup in slow motion, his hands on her small waist. He lifted her up toward the net like a ballerina, and some of the girls gasped at their effortless dance. In that moment, it was Rachel, not Jenna, who sank the basket, Rachel whose shoulder Father squeezed, whose hair he ruffled. "Anybody else want to give it a try?" Father asked, grinning and rubbing his hands together. I broke into an icy sweat. Shivering, I looked at my shoes and hid behind my heavy bangs. I made myself as small as possible, so small I could have slipped between the wooden floorboards.

---

Adolescence is an endurance test. Almost everyone makes it through, but in every class, there are a few casualties. Not being one of them is an achievement in itself. In school, most girls strategize in the same way a long-distance runner situates herself, jockeying for position, then holding her spot until late in the race when she might find an opening and make a move. It's safest to be in the middle of the pack, on the outside edge.

I made the honor roll, but just barely. In concert band, I played third clarinet, never first. I ate lunch with girls like me, girls who sat unnoticed at the far end of the cafeteria. We were quiet, unimpressive girls—not student council reps or cheerleaders. We were nothing like the girls in movies who swear to stay in touch when they go off to college and promise to be bridesmaids at each other's weddings. We were friends of convenience who shared homework assignments and speculated about our teachers' private lives. We talked about the boys in our classes—who was the cutest, who was the nicest. We stood together at school dances like a stand of saplings. A few girls went steady with Good Catholic Boys—clean-cut boys their parents liked more than they did. We were all sure we would marry the first boy we kissed, the first boy who paid us any attention. I knew what was expected from girls who go with Good Catholic Boys. I knew I would say yes from the start. *Yes* at the movies, behind the arena, in his parents' car. I knew, when the time came, I would say yes without uttering a sound. *Yes, yes, yes.* A boy in my history class told me he liked me, that I was smart and funny and cool. A few days later when I passed him in the hall, he and his friends mooed like cows, then laughed hysterically. I pretended not to hear. I shrugged it off and pushed it from my mind, but it stung like vinegar in an open cut.

By fifteen, I was hiding behind my glasses and frizzy hair. I pulled my shoulders forward and wrapped a scarf around my throat three times. I gained weight. Ten pounds, then twenty, then more. The new layers were a distraction, a blanket, a buffer. I lay in bed and stroked the cellulite on my upper arms and thighs, and the dimpled flesh rippled beneath my fingertips. I wore the same hoodie and sweatpants every day. I even slept in them. I was never completely naked. I washed only out of necessity—armpits one day, hair another. My mother encouraged, cajoled, and bribed. "You're such a pretty girl," she'd say. "Tie that hair back out of your face. Maybe try a little lip gloss." She gave me money to buy new clothes, to go to the mall and get my nails done. She made appointments with the doctor and filled the freezer with Lean Cuisines. Almost daily I said, "I'm okay, I'm fine." And the more I said it, the more I believed it.

For so long, I saw but did not see. I heard but did not hear. I did just enough to keep my parents at bay, to avoid attracting attention. Avoidance and denial served me well. Until they didn't.

---

The year I turned sixteen, a girl in my class took a skipping rope from the equipment room in the gym, wound it tightly around her neck, and hanged herself from a hook in the girls' changing room. I heard about it on the school bus the morning after it happened. Rumors churned like white-water rapids. *Didn't she date that skinny guy with the red hair?… I think he dumped her.…*

*Someone said she was pregnant.... Yeah, she had an abortion.... She was anorexic, for sure. Everyone knew.... Her parents got divorced, and her dad moved to the States. She had a lot of issues.*

But what no one would have said, even if they'd known, was that she was not the only sad, tortured girl, that so many of us would have done the same thing if we'd been weaker. Or stronger. I'm not sure which. What they couldn't see was that she was magnificently reckless and wildly brave. A girl Icarus.

What they would never understand was that girls like her were tempted all the time. We picked our toenails to the quick and peeled the delicate skin until they bled. We plucked hairs from our heads and created secret bald spots the size of quarters. We stole pills and laxatives from our grandmothers' medicine chests. We binged and purged long into the night. We sliced our inner thighs with razor blades and watched the blood trickle and clot. We swigged Robitussin and Listerine and huffed Liquid Paper. We survived the only way we knew how.

---

My parents' concern was relentless. *You're not yourself. You're pale. You're not well. Your grades are slipping. You never leave your room. What on earth is wrong with you?* There was no way to answer their questions. My classmate's suicide had created a dangerous undertow, and I could barely stay afloat.

Finally, late one evening, after Rachel was in bed and we were alone, I broke. I told them about Father, about what he'd done, where and when, how long it had gone on. They stared open-mouthed, and their eyes reddened. They took it in as best they could, tried to swallow it in one huge gulp, then choked and spat. They were shocked and guilty, incredulous and eviscerated. If they had questions, they were too stunned to ask.

They blamed themselves and begged my forgiveness. *Mea culpa! Mea culpa!*

"I'm sorry," I said, then I ran upstairs, locked my bedroom door, and burrowed under the covers. I hadn't known what to expect. I knew they would be upset, but I was stunned by their apologies. I was the one who should have apologized. I had been lying to them for so long, avoiding the truth and keeping secrets. I'd never said a word about the things Father did all those times he tucked me in, when I helped at the rectory, when he cornered me in the schoolyard. I could have stopped it years ago, and I didn't. I was so stupid, so weak. I covered my ears and screamed into my pillow. Just then, I felt a hand on my back. I looked up, and Rachel was standing beside the bed. "What's the matter?" she asked.

I froze, then quickly wiped my face on my sleeve. "It's okay. I'm okay. I just had a bad dream. How about I tuck you back into bed?" I took her hand and led her to her room. She had left her Strawberry Shortcake lamp on and the room glowed pink. Once she was under the covers, I reached to turn out the light.

"Mom says I'm too old to keep a light on at night. But I like it," Rachel said, yawning.

"Well, nine's not *that* old," I said, folding the quilt under her chin. "Maybe you'll want it off when you're ten. Night night." I leaned in to kiss her cheek, and she was already asleep. I sat on the edge of her bed for a few more minutes. She looked so small, so innocent. I envied her.

When I got back to my room, my parents were still downstairs. I could hear only snatches of their conversation: *My God, she was five, younger than Rachel, too young to know...right under our noses.... Why didn't she come to us?* And I wondered for a fleeting second if maybe they could be at fault, just a little. I laid awake and listened as they wept and cursed and raged late into the night.

The next morning, they phoned the Bishop. We drove an hour to his office, where we sat on fine leather chairs. The Bishop leaned across his desk, his pale blue eyes searching. "I've just spoken with Father on the telephone, and he's concerned. Very concerned. It seems there's been a miscommunication, that she misread his intentions. Our priests are human too. They're young, some of them, and we do our best to help them develop their pastoral skills. But sometimes the stress, their desire to help, can create... situations. We're all *very* concerned. I will deal with this personally. It won't happen again. You have my word."

At the end of the meeting, my parents signed some papers. "This is standard. For your daughter's protection," the Bishop told them. "This matter will be handled confidentially, and then you can put it behind you. The financial compensation is for your time and distress. It never should have come to this." As we were leaving, my parents shook the Bishop's hand.

We drove home in silence. My parents stared straight ahead. I rested my head on the window and watched the blur of mile markers. I was filled with regret and desperate for my bed. All I could think was *Why did I tell?* I knew it had been a mistake. My confession was twisted and ugly. I felt like I had committed a horrible sin, that I had unleashed a contagion that had infected us all. *Mea maxima culpa.* There was no absolution for this confession, no balm for my guilt.

On a Saturday morning about two weeks later, I woke late. The house was silent, and I went down to the kitchen and poured myself a bowl of Corn Flakes. My parents had left the newspaper on the table, open to an article announcing Father's transfer. I knew they had left it for me to see. I shoved my breakfast aside. My heart raced as I read. Father was to be the new pastor of the parish on the other side of the city, the one that looks more like a casino than a church. Father would arrive just in time for the old Monsignor to retire. He planned to start a family council and a youth group.

Most people reading the paper would see Father as a breath of fresh air for that church. I could picture his new parishioners greeting him with smiles and casseroles. The article was accompanied by a photo of Father grinning widely, his eyes clear and bright with the hope of a new beginning.

I went back to bed, my cereal untouched. Eventually my heartbeat slowed, but my chest stayed tight all day, aching with shame and regret.

# [PART 2]

A secret is a mustard seed, a tiny speck with the potential to grow a million times its size. Clench it in your fist and never let it see the light. Feel it quiver with potential energy, like a Mexican jumping bean.

A secret is a little red firecracker, the kind children are told never to carry in their pockets. *See the burns on that boy? He was playing with firecrackers.* Secrets are like that—the tiniest spark, and it's game over. They are compact blasting caps, which, if detonated, can bring down a fifty-story building. Pause to imagine the latent possibility.

A secret is powerful yet invisible, like a germ. Scientists discovered the bacteria that caused the Black Plague, a medieval secret that wiped out a third of the population. That they still exist is no surprise; people are mortal, but secrets are eternal.

A secret is a life sentence, a permanent gag order more effective than duct tape across the mouth. People who keep secrets are hog-tied, immobilized. A secret is a straitjacket laced with chains; when Houdini asked to be submerged in a tank of water, it wasn't to make his escape more difficult, but to quiet the screaming of his skin.

A secret is a suit of armor, like chain mail under your clothes. It weighs you down and keeps you safe. Wear it like a bulletproof vest. If the words are not said aloud, you will be protected and impervious to doubt, ridicule, and worse: pity.

If you keep the secret, it will stay contained and containable. It is impossible to say what will happen if it gets out. The Pandora's box hidden under your bed is full of terrible knowledge that will change everything. Still your trembling hands, seal the lid with tape and elastic bands, and place it in the bottom of the trash can.

Secrets can be kept so long that silence becomes second nature. Close your mouth and your mind. Seal them off with paraffin wax. *The Seal of the Confessional.* Keep the secret, even from yourself. Dress in the dark. Camouflage yourself in oversized hoodies and black yoga pants. Play music so loudly your body vibrates. When you are able to sleep, bury your head under your pillow and clench your teeth.

Telling will change how you see and are seen, will define you in ways you cannot predict and do not recognize. *No one likes a tattletale, a snitch, a rat.* Whispered confessions will require new words. Cleanly enunciated, vulgar verbs. *Fondle. Grope. Penetrate. Sodomize. Rape.*

If you dare, tell just one person, that person who will never, ever repeat what you say. Barely whisper it. Just mouth the words. *This thing happened to me. I was four or six or eight. It just kept happening. I couldn't stop it. I didn't know how. It was so fucked up. I was so fucked up.*

When you confide in that one person, you will be flayed and lifted up at the same time. Tell until there is nothing left: not words, not anger, not breath. Tell *everything*. Scream until you lose your voice or your mind. When you finally inhale, it will be like your first infant breath. Lie on your back and stare at the ceiling. Feel the air in your lungs and think, *Okay. Okay.* Telling is an end and a beginning.

# [1985–1987]

For weeks after graduation, I scanned the classified ads and applied for every job I had even a slim chance of getting. I'd managed to avoid my parents' pleas to apply to university, convincing them I wanted to take a year off. *To travel,* I told them. *To work. To figure out what I want to do.* I couldn't go and couldn't explain why. They didn't believe me, but they gave me space. Maybe space was all they had to give. The relationship between us was on uneven ground, and it was all we could do to maintain our footing. We lived in the same house and ate at the same table, ignoring the uncomfortable tension between us. Rachel seemed oblivious to it all, and her cheeriness was a blessing. Dinners were spent listening to the details of Rachel's day and her plans with her friends. An outsider would never have known anything was amiss. Sometimes, I resented my parents, their determination to move on, to put the past in the past. More than anything, I wanted them to ask if I wanted to talk about it, even though I would have said no and changed the subject. Over time, I came to accept the strained silence. It was part of the tacit agreement we'd established two years before, the day I'd told them about Father. So I kept up my end of the deal and never said a word.

Though my skin crawled and my stomach churned, I continued to go to mass with my parents and Rachel on Sundays. Then I found a pill bottle in my parents' medicine cabinet. Under Mother's name were the instructions: "Take as needed to manage nervous stress." I began stealing the little pink pills, just one each week before church, which made sitting in the pew a little easier. One Sunday, I saw a ONE DAY AT A TIME bumper sticker on a car in the church parking lot. *That's it exactly*, I thought, *just one day, one hour at a time.*

When I finally landed an interview for a receptionist job at a busy real estate office, Holmes Realty, I thought it was a long shot. I hadn't gone to secretarial school and knew nothing about real estate. I showed up for the interview wearing my best skirt and blouse, my hair twisted into compliance with dozens of bobby pins. Mr. Holmes was there, but he said little more than "Lovely to meet you" and "You'll hear from us soon." The interview was conducted by Mrs. Best, who had been the office receptionist for twenty-five years and would soon retire. My control-top pantyhose impeded normal breathing, but I managed to answer Mrs. Best's questions about typing (*Yes, forty words per minute.*) and organization (*Oh yes, very organized. I did filing in my dad's insurance office last summer*...). When Mr. Holmes called a few days later to offer me the job, I was surprised and grateful to have somewhere to go each day. Mostly, I was relieved for my parents. They wouldn't have to explain to their friends why I wasn't off at school with my classmates, and I wouldn't be "wasting my life" reading novels or watching television.

The real estate agents looked every bit as perfect as their photos on benches and billboards: bright and glossy, all blond updos and lip gloss, chiselled jawlines and silk ties. I saw them the way I would a display of designer shoes in a department store window: desirable, but clearly out of reach. I didn't want to be them so much as be near them, close enough that some of their unselfconscious ease might rub off. I looked the same as I had in high school, minus the school-girl uniform, with my unruly hair and slightly-too-thick glasses. Having me in the office ensured that the agents would appear shiny and polished by comparison, even on their worst days. I stocked their offices with pens and paperclips, brewed pot after pot of coffee, and made sure their open house flyers, lawn signs, and paperwork were ready before they asked. *You're a gem!* they'd say as they breezed in and out of the office, never pausing to make eye contact. I was chameleon-like, practiced at the art of invisibility. It took most of them months to learn my name.

I went to work, came home, then did it all again the next day. I seldom thought about the past. I remembered in my body, but not in my mind. And when my pulse quickened and my ears started to buzz, I'd sneak a pink pill. The relief they provided was worth the risk that my mother would notice. If she did, she didn't say a word.

---

I had been working for almost a year when Mr. Holmes called me into his office. "When you have a minute," he said. *What have I done?* I wondered. His office was at the back of the building, and by the time I reached the door, I had convinced myself I would be fired, though I had no clue why.

"Come in, come in. Sit," he said. I perched on the edge of the chair and folded my hands in my lap. "You've been with us a year now, is that right?"

I nodded, afraid to speak in case I started to cry.

"What are you doing for lunch?" he asked.

"Well, uh, I usually eat at my desk, in case the phone rings. But I can eat in the staff room if that would be better."

Mr. Holmes smiled. "That's not what I meant. I want to take you out for lunch, to celebrate your first year with the company. Would Friday be okay?"

"Sure! I mean, thank you. Yes, Friday is fine." My original unease morphed into a whole new variety of apprehension.

"Perfect! Let's say noon, then."

I walked back to my desk, jittery with thoughts of spending an entire lunch hour with Mr. Holmes but also pleased he had thought about me.

Before I had taken more than a few bites of my chicken salad sandwich, Mr. Holmes invited me to dinner. We had been talking about our favorite foods. It seemed Mr. Holmes—or Neil, as he insisted I call him—had been to every restaurant in the city. He raved about foods I'd never heard of: tandoori chicken and gyros and Korean barbecue. I had been only to the three restaurants my parents took us to: Maria's Diner for bacon and eggs after church, and The Ritz Steakhouse and Red Lobster for special birthday dinners. "You mean you've never tried the pizza at Enzo's? You have to go! What's tomorrow? Saturday? Are you free?" And that was how I ended up on what felt like a date with Neil.

I noticed his shoes right away. They were soft brown suede, the color of cocoa. He looked at least ten years younger outside the office. And it wasn't just because he wore jeans instead of a suit.

It was the way he leaned toward me across the booth, eager and attentive. "I'm so glad you were available on short notice," he said. "I know you'll love the pizza here." And as he spoke—about his love of pizza, his failed attempts to make his own dough, his passion for Italian cooking—I found myself unexpectedly calm. I didn't have to think about what to say or when to laugh or where to look. I hadn't been asked so many questions in years. Maybe ever. His questions were not like the ones teachers asked when you were daydreaming and they tried to catch you off guard, the kind that made me whither and sweat. These felt like gentle nudges, prodding me to tell just a little, then a little more, then a little more. *Do you like to ice skate? What kind of music do you listen to? Where were you when John Lennon died? What's your favorite movie? Have you seen* Out of Africa*? What did you think of it? Do you use the public library much? What do you like to read? Tell me about that pendant you're wearing? Have you ever been to Vancouver? Where would you go if you could go anywhere in the world? Do you like roller coasters? Two-in-one shampoo? Crossword puzzles? Do you have brothers and sisters? What was your best subject in school? Do you ever think about going to college one day? What would you study?* His questions held up a mirror, not to force a glaring reflection but to offer an indirect glimpse of my better side, the side I wouldn't allow myself to see.

I found myself telling Neil things I hadn't told anyone, like how I'd always loved English, and how I didn't know if I would go to college, but if I did, I would maybe try creative writing. He asked about my favorite writers and what kinds of books I enjoyed. It was ten o'clock when loud music intruded on our conversation. The lights had dimmed, and the bar was filling up. Neil leaned across the table and shouted, "Sorry if I've asked too many questions. I'm not usually so pushy."

"It's okay," I said. "You're easy to talk to. I've had a really good time."

"Should we go? We can have another drink here, if you'd like. Or we could walk...."

We left the restaurant and strolled along the main street, pausing to look at window displays. When we passed Holmes Realty, he told me about his parents and how they started the business. "Dad had a great sense of humor," he said. "He always joked, 'With a name like Holmes, I knew I'd be a detective or a realtor!' He was a kind, kind person. Mom, too. They came from England after the war. They were so proud of their business, always interested in their employees and their families. Dad's been gone four years now, and Mom died six months after. I never thought I'd work in the business, but here I am. But it's good, you know? Finding homes for people."

"What would you have done if you hadn't stayed here?" I asked.

"When I was in high school, I guess I thought I'd be an actor or a director. I moved to Toronto right out of college. I got a few acting jobs, but mostly, I worked as an usher. It sounds silly now...." Neil's voice trailed off, and I couldn't tell if his memories of that time were happy or sad. "Then when Dad got sick, I came back to help out. I'm where I'm supposed to be. Now how about that nightcap? My house is just around the corner."

"I, um, I can't really...I didn't tell my parents I'd be late. Not that I have to report in! But they like me to go to church with them in the morning, you know? And I...." I clenched my jaw to keep from stammering on and stared at my feet.

"Oh my God, I'm so sorry," Neil said. "I didn't mean to suggest...I mean, I wouldn't...I really meant a drink. Just a drink. Honest!"

"It's okay. A drink would be great. Maybe another time, though."

"Let me walk you home at least," Neil offered, but I had already turned away.

"I don't live far. It's fine. I'll see you Monday." I walked to the end of the block, then turned the corner and began to run, my sandals slapping the sidewalk. I knew I was being ridiculous, that Neil was harmless, but I couldn't get home quickly enough.

Despite my awkward exit, Neil continued to ask me to join him for dinners on Saturday nights: Enzo's led to Golden Thai, which led to Korean Fusion. When my parents asked about my plans, I didn't mention I was going with Neil, just that people from work were getting together. Neil and I were becoming friends, and I didn't want my parents to think there was anything more between us. At first, even I was surprised that Neil enjoyed spending time with me. But as the weeks passed, I got the sense that he didn't have many friends in the city, and with his parents gone, he was lonely. I could relate: Although my parents were alive and well, I felt like I'd lost something too.

One evening in late September, we feasted on spanakopita, dolmades, tzatziki, and warm pita at a little Greek place I didn't know existed, though I had lived in the city my entire life. We sat on its courtyard patio under hundreds of tiny, blue lights, talking until late in the evening, leaving only when we realized we were keeping the waitstaff from closing up. We walked for a while, and when we decided to go to Neil's place for a drink, this time it didn't feel strange at all.

He lived in his parents' house, a stately brick Georgian, shaded by huge maple trees. As we walked from the front foyer to the kitchen, I was struck by the contrast between Neil and his home. The flocked wallpaper, the overstuffed floral living room suite, the shiny linoleum in the kitchen preserved his parents' style and taste. As Neil poured drinks, I glanced around at the green gingham curtains, the ceramic napkin holder and matching salt and pepper shakers, the BLESS THIS HOUSE trivet on the stovetop. Clearly, he had not changed a thing.

"I know," he said. "I need to update the place. It's just hard to picture it any other way."

"It's homey," I said, leaning against the yellow Formica counter.

"Let me show you the rest of the house." Neil walked through the kitchen into a family room with a stone fireplace and large picture windows onto the backyard. Also on the main floor was an office panelled in dark oak, and upstairs were three spacious bedrooms and a bathroom with a claw-foot tub. "This is my room," Neil said. I stood in the doorway and could see that this room had been redecorated, with modern furniture and built-in bookcases across the widest wall. The bed was topped with a thick gray duvet, and a tower of books sat on the nightstand.

"Now this looks like you," I said.

"I spend a lot of time up here," he said. "Anyway, let's go have that drink."

As we turned to go, I noticed a photo on the dresser. Neil and a man about his age, standing on a dock. Neil's arm rested on the man's shoulder, and they were laughing at something or someone outside the frame. "Who's this?" I asked, picking it up for a closer look.

"That's my friend, Marcus. He died last year. That picture was taken a couple summers ago, in the Muskokas."

"I'm so sorry," I said. I was sorry for Neil and sorry I had asked.

"Thanks," Neil whispered. And as I placed the photo back on the dresser, I could hear his quick steps on the stairs.

I couldn't have known on that first visit how much time—how many hours, days, months, years—I would spend in that house.

I continued visiting after our dinners out, sometimes for a drink, sometimes coffee and dessert. Soon Neil began cooking for me—homemade gnocchi one week, chicken cacciatore the next. We sat at the kitchen table and talked late into the night. We never ran out of things to say, never tired of each other's company. In a way, he was like the big brother I'd never had, and I never felt pressure to tell him anything I didn't want him to know. Our friendship allowed me to curate a new version of myself, a more confident version, free from the worst parts of the past. Even when our conversations cut a little too close to the bone—when he asked about my relationship with my parents or why I hadn't gone to college—I felt safe with Neil, safe in his house.

It was during the heat of July when Neil first called in sick. I was at my desk reviewing the realtors' schedules for the day when he phoned. He said he was feeling "under the weather" and would work from home. A few days later, he called to ask if I would bring his phone messages and some paperwork to the house. "Just let yourself in," he said. "The back door is open. You can set everything on the kitchen table. Just leave it and go. I wouldn't want you to catch anything."

When I arrived, I was surprised at the state of the kitchen. Dirty dishes lined the counter, a pot of congealed soup sat on the stovetop, and there was a small puddle of what looked like orange juice on the floor in front of the fridge. I called to him, quietly at first. "Neil? Are you here?" Silence. I stood at the bottom of the stairs and said his name a bit louder. When he didn't answer, I went up. He didn't hear me enter his room. The air was still and sour. He was in a deep sleep, his breath raspy. One arm hung over the edge of the bed, and his legs were tangled in perspiration-soaked sheets. I said his name again and placed my hand gently on his forehead. "Neil, can you hear me?"

His eyes fluttered.

"Neil?"

Several seconds passed, and then his eyes came into focus. "You're here," he whispered, his voice gritty and strained.

"I think you need to see a doctor," I said.

"No. No, I'm getting better, I think." He tried to sit up. "Could you please get me a glass of water?"

As I waited for the water in the bathroom sink to run cold, I took in the damp towels on the floor, the pill bottles and their contents strewn across the countertop. I wondered if I should call someone. But who?

When I returned to Neil's bedside, he had propped himself on the headboard. He had lost weight, and his skin had a yellow cast. "I bet I look like hell," he said, smiling.

"Well, I've seen you look better." I winked and handed him the glass. He took a sip. "Drink more," I said. "You're probably dehydrated."

"Yeah. I think I had a fever."

"Have you seen a doctor? You've been sick a few days."

"I have. Seen the doctor, I mean. A while ago. I'm pretty sure this is just a passing thing. I'm feeling better. Really."

In that moment, Neil looked so desperate, so exposed. I worried that if I asked too many questions, he might shut me out. He had let me into his life. I knew he had boundaries, and I didn't want to make him uncomfortable. But I knew he needed help.

"Could you eat something?" I asked. "Maybe a piece of toast...."

He agreed to the toast, ate a few bites, then fell asleep. I ran back to the office, sorted the day's mail, and left a note telling the agents I was working from Neil's home office. When I returned, he had changed his pajamas and was reading in bed. "See? Better already," he said.

We chatted for a few minutes about work, then I went downstairs and cleaned up the kitchen. I found a carton of Bolognese sauce in the freezer and took it out to thaw for supper, then I phoned my mother and told her I'd be working late.

Neil returned to the office the following week, as cheerful as ever. No one commented on the change in his appearance, but I couldn't have been the only one to notice how thin he had become. He continued to call in sick, a day here and there every few weeks, then more and more frequently. I often ran files to and from the office so he could work at home. Our Saturday dinners out became takeout meals, and as he became weaker, I did my best to cook simple dinners in his kitchen after work. He coached me through passable efforts at stroganoff and lasagna, and we joked about my failed attempts at pancakes. *Coasters? Hubcaps? Frisbees!* I drove him to doctors' appointments, picked up his prescriptions at the pharmacy, and laid out a complicated medication regimen on the bathroom vanity. By the end of the summer, Neil had stopped coming into the office altogether. I went in for an hour or so in the morning and again in the afternoon, when a nurse came to the house to change Neil's IV. Our routines evolved with minimal discussion, without permissions or the need for explanation. "What would I do without you?" Neil asked.

I took this opening to pose a question I'd been wanting to ask for a while. "I was wondering, if there was ever an emergency, or a time when you get really sick, is there someone I should call?"

Neil's smile faded. "Not really. I mean, I don't have any close relatives. And my friends are mostly far away, or gone."

I regretted asking. "It's okay," I said quickly. "I just wanted to be sure."

"You're a godsend, you know."

What he didn't know was that he was helping me too. I had never been so busy, or felt so needed.

As the days grew shorter, I began to sleep at Neil's house in a guest bedroom. I still went home for dinner every few days, mostly to see Rachel. In as few words as possible, I explained to my parents that Neil was ill. "I'm his personal assistant," I told them. "It's easier if I'm there to manage everything." I was shocked at their ready acceptance of this new arrangement. Maybe it was easier for them if I wasn't around. When I was with them, all the unsaid things between us hung in the air like heavy fog, and there was no sign of it lifting.

When Neil's pain increased and he needed medication every few hours through the night, I slept in his room, in a recliner his nurse and I had moved up from the den. Before long, I began to lie beside him in the early evenings as he drifted in and out of sleep. We spooned, and I felt every vertebra, his heartbeat absorbed by my breasts. We laid face to face and interlaced our fingers, his metallic breath mingling with mine. When he woke in the night, I rubbed cocoa butter on the knobs of his elbows and knees and ran my fingers through his thinning hair. I eased him into the bath and bundled sweat-drenched sheets into the washer. I used Q-tips to apply salve to the purple lesions on his arms and torso. He had good days, and we watched movies and played Scrabble; he had bad days and didn't speak. We celebrated his thirty-seventh birthday with turtle cheesecake and champagne.

Our life together was a tender, fading thing, but its rhythms soothed me. Good days, then bad, then good. Fevered nights, followed by calm mornings. The way I could ease his pain, even a little, with simple remedies and the touch of my hands. I focused on these things—not on the past or the future, not on diagnoses or prognoses, not on what I might do years down the road, but what I could do that day. *Today,* I thought, *I can do this much.*

Early one January morning, Neil was sleeping soundly, so I crept downstairs, made a pot of coffee, and brought in the newspaper. I poured a cup and unfolded the paper. The oversized headline read: *Priest Charged with Child Sexual Abuse*. Without reading further, I knew the priest was Father. The words echoed in my head like a thunderclap. I stared at the headline. It stretched like caution tape across the table—and across kitchen tables all over the country, across every newspaper kiosk in every bus depot, corner store, hospital, hotel lobby, and country club. It would be the first thing my parents saw that morning, the talk of everyone I ever knew. It would be the lead story on drive-time radio and morning television, the topic of discussion at coffee shops, at every greasy spoon in every town, at every rest stop on every highway. Students on college campuses would rail in disgust. Old women in hair salons would *tsk-tsk* their disapproval. Presbyterians and Baptists, Jews and Muslims, Hindus and Sikhs would raise their voices in condemnation. Everyone everywhere would have a claim on the story, on the truths and falsehoods they read between the lines. Everyone everywhere would know what I knew.

Neil stood in the kitchen doorway in a white T-shirt and pajama pants, leaning on his IV pole. "Did you know him?" he asked.

"Geez, you scared me!" I said. "What are you doing out of bed?"

"I thought I'd come down for breakfast. So, did you? Know him?" His dark eyes searched mine, and I looked away.

"Oh, yeah, I…I think so," I said, fumbling as I tried to refold the paper. "Let's get you back upstairs—or at least get your robe. You must be freezing."

I chattered on and on, all the way up the stairs, about the snow that had fallen overnight, about whether he would like scrambled eggs or oatmeal, about the nurse's visit that morning. Neil was winded by the time we reached his room, and he eased himself onto the bed and closed his eyes. "I'll be right back with breakfast," I said and ran downstairs.

When I reached the kitchen, I stopped to catch my breath. Neil's question had caught me off guard. As close as we had become, there were things I wasn't ready to tell him—or anyone. I stared at the folded newspaper. I couldn't read the article. Not now. Not yet. I feared my mother might call, so I took the phone off the hook. I put some oats on to simmer and set Neil's breakfast tray, then I stood at the counter and stared out the window. The glare off the snow made my eyes water. It erased the yard, the fence, the garden shed. I closed my eyes and the scorching white spread inward, flooding my brain, coursing down my spine, running like quicksilver in my veins. When I opened my eyes, my hands and arms glowed bright white against the stainless-steel sink in an unholy Transfiguration.

The lid on the pot rattled as the porridge bubbled over, and in my rush to pull it from the stove, I burned my hand. I dropped the pot in the sink and stared at the burn as it turned from pink to garish purple, and aqueous blisters rose under the skin. The pain was a relief, a distraction so complete I didn't hear Chris, one of Neil's home care nurses, let herself in. She held my shoulders and steered me toward a chair. "Let me take a look at that burn," she said.

I nodded slowly, like an obedient child. I watched Chris clean the burn. As my head cleared, the pain increased, but I didn't wince as she applied an ointment and wrapped my hand in sterile gauze. *She must think I'm incompetent*, I thought. *She knows I can't take care of myself, let alone Neil.*

"I'm sorry," I whispered.

"It's not your fault," Chris replied. "These things happen. Keep it covered, and I'll check it and change the dressing when I'm here for Neil's appointments. It's going to be sore for a while, I'm afraid. But it should ease up in a couple days."

"It's not so bad," I said. I don't know why I downplayed the pain, why I felt I needed to lie. I was good at evading the truth, accomplished in the art of denial.

Chris remade Neil's breakfast and took it upstairs. I rose slowly from the chair, put the phone back on the cradle, and began tidying the kitchen with one hand. I put the newspaper in the recycling bin beside the refrigerator, then pulled it out and took it to the living room, out of sight. *I'll read it later*, I thought. I couldn't tell if that was a lie or the truth.

---

The next day, I mustered the courage to read the article. And then I read it again. And again. It transported Father back into my life. He was everywhere. I saw his shiny black shoes in Neil's closet, the back of his head on the city bus. His black overcoat brushed past on the street, and I gasped. His bushy eyebrows and sour breath sat down beside me in the doctor's waiting room, and I shifted to another chair. I heard his laugh in the video store and ducked behind a display. I cringed as his hand reached across the counter at the pharmacy. I knew my eyes were playing tricks, that I was the only one who could see Father. But no matter how quickly I moved, I could never avoid his shadow.

---

I tried to schedule nurses' visits on Sunday mornings so I could join my parents and Rachel for mass. I knew this kept my parents happy, and it was the easiest way to spend time with them without having a conversation. In the weeks after the newspaper article was published, I didn't have enough energy or courage to discuss what I knew we were all thinking about. Not that we'd ever talked about it. And I missed them, especially Rachel. Mostly I went to see her, to sit beside her in the pew and hold her hand during the

Lord's Prayer. For those few minutes, I could close my eyes and be anywhere, alone with Rachel.

Then one afternoon, Rachel showed up at Neil's house. "Hey! Come in!" I said before I could even open the screen door.

"That's okay," Rachel replied. "I can't stay."

"Step in out of the cold at least," I said, opening the door wider.

Rachel looked at her shoes. "Um, Mom said maybe I shouldn't stay. That Mr. Holmes is probably sleeping."

I knew immediately what that meant. "I suppose Mom's afraid you'll catch something from Neil, which is completely ridiculous. He's had pneumonia for weeks now, and I haven't caught it. His immune system is compromised. We're more dangerous to him than he is to us. Besides, he's upstairs sleeping. Just come into the kitchen."

Rachel hesitated for about half a second, then stepped in and kicked her boots onto the mat. "I brought you a couple books," she said, reaching into her backpack. "Your old copy of *Pride and Prejudice* and the new Stephen King."

"That's perfect," I said. I was so happy to see her that I just sat and stared.

"So...how's it going here?" Rachel glanced around the tidy kitchen.

"It's okay. I mean, Neil hasn't been doing well, so I don't go into the office very often. But I can do some work at home—here. And the office is so organized, they're fine without me, really.... How are *you*? Do you have finals coming up?"

"Yeah, last week of January. Ms. Castillo's math exam is going to be brutal, but otherwise, it'll be fine."

"You'll ace them all. You always do," I said.

Rachel smiled. "Yeah, I guess." She folded her hands on the table in front of her and said, "So, um...I just wanted to ask you if everything is okay. I mean, with us. Like, I know you're here to take care of Mr. Holmes, but you used to come home for supper once in a while. And I just wondered if you were kind of avoiding us."

"Oh, God. No, Rach. No. I'm not avoiding you at all. Like I said, Neil's been really sick, and I hate to leave in case he needs anything."

Rachel stared at her hands. "It's just, for the past few weeks, since that article in the paper…it's been weird. At first, Mom did that thing where she cleans day and night. And when there was nothing left to clean, she started baking. The freezer is packed full of cookies and tarts, like it's Christmas. It's insane. And then, the other day, I heard Mom and Dad talking about the article. I couldn't hear much, but they seemed really upset. I know that priest used to come to our house…."

"Do you remember him?" I asked, my heart rate climbing.

"Sure. I remember he came for dinner sometimes. I would have been four, maybe five. He used to tuck us in."

"Yeah. He did." My heart raced and my throat tightened.

"Mom said something about feeling guilty. About how they should have known. It was like she *knew* something, like maybe she knew about what a perv Father was, way before the article came out."

I took a deep breath. Then another. Then another. *Say it,* I told myself. *Say it. Say it. Say it. Say it. Say it. Say it….*

Rachel placed her hand on my arm. "I read the article. It didn't mention the girls' names, but they were girls from our grade school, girls who were there when you were, in the seventies. It said there are eight of them so far, but they expect more will come forward. A lot more."

I wanted to tell Rachel. I knew what I wanted to say, but how could I say it in a way that wouldn't change everything between us? I couldn't bear the thought of Rachel knowing. I was just about to make an excuse, to say I had to check on Neil and give him his medication, when the afternoon nurse knocked and let herself in. I introduced her to Rachel, and she went upstairs.

I stood and walked toward the door. "Thanks for coming, Rach. It was so good to see you. I miss you, you know." We hugged in the doorway for a long time.

Rachel knew, and I didn't have to say the words.

I was tormented by memories. They descended like a plague. Worse than boils on my skin. Worse than locusts. Much worse than darkness. As soon as I left one behind, another surged forward and overtook me. Often they came at night, but they sometimes crept in in the daytime too, when I was on the city bus or washing dishes. It was as though each remembered incident had happened yesterday, this morning, five minutes ago. I could smell the scent of that place and of Father, and it made my eyes water.... *I'm small, small enough to be lifted onto his lap. He teases me about my braids. "Piggy tales," he says, laughing. And I laugh too. He pretends to bite the bows on the end of each braid, his hot breath dangerously close. He rubs my back through my sundress, the one with the pink and white daisies. "Feels nice, doesn't it?" he says, and I try to smile. I want to be good, so I sit very still and nod my head. I do not make a sound. I'm silent, even when I want to scream.*

I thought less about Father as Neil's care consumed me. Nurses came to the house three times a day to change Neil's IV bag and flush the access port on his chest. I had often used this time to go to the office or run a quick errand, but as his health worsened, I didn't leave unless it was necessary.

One evening, I was sitting in the kitchen when Chris came downstairs. Chris was Neil's favorite nurse for her skill with the IV needle and her sense of humor. I liked her too. She always took time to answer my questions and show me the best ways to manage Neil's increasingly complicated care. "He's sleeping," Chris said. "I think I tired him out."

"The last few days he's been sleeping a lot," I told her.

"That's normal." Chris set her bag on the floor and eased herself into the chair opposite me. "Jesus, it feels good to get off my feet."

"Can I get you a coffee?" I asked.

"Maybe a glass of water. I've been meaning to talk to you about a few things."

I set the water in front of her and waited while she took a long drink. "I know you understand how sick Neil is and that he's not going to get better. These cases always progress faster than you think." She took another drink, and I refilled her glass. "So, what you need to know is, he can't go to the hospital, no matter what happens. When he's in crisis, your first thought will be to call 9-1-1, but don't."

"I know he doesn't want to go to the hospital. He told me he wants to stay at home," I said.

"He *can't* go, honey. Not ever. They'll put him in isolation, and hospital policy is that only immediate family can visit. That means you won't be allowed in. You could try telling them you're his sister, but they'll want proof. And when he's in there, in isolation, he won't get much care. There's some nurses who won't even go in the room; they just leave meds and food at the door. I've seen it. It's criminal, really, but that's how it is." She cleared her throat. "So, here's my number." She handed me a slip of paper with her name and phone number scrawled in black ink. "You call me *anytime*. Day or night, it doesn't matter. If he falls and you need help, or he's in too much pain, or if something else happens and you don't know what to do, you call."

I nodded, grateful for her kindness and nervous about what was ahead.

"If I can't come," Chris said, "I'll send someone. There's a group of us women, we've been doing this for a while now. Some are nurses, a few are doctors, most are just good women who know what to do. They'll come. The thing with AIDS patients is you can't count on the system. These gay men are treated like second-class citizens. It's messed up, but that's the truth."

I thanked her, and she squeezed my hand. "Take care, honey. I'll see you tomorrow."

As the door closed behind her, Chris's words lingered. *The thing with AIDS patients....* It was the first time I had heard it said aloud, and I was overcome with relief. For months, doctors and nurses had discussed Neil's weight loss and T-cell count, his lesions and recurring pneumonia, but no one had said AIDS. Not once. I knew, of course. He had every sign and symptom. But we never said the word, as though saying it would make it real, as though one syllable held the power to reduce Neil to his disease.

I climbed the stairs to his room and stood over him. In many ways, he was unrecognizable. He had shrivelled to half his size. His skin was translucent, and his hair had thinned to mere wisps. Blue veins stretched across his skull. I put my hand on his forehead. "Neil," I whispered, "Neil...."

Several seconds later, his eyes fluttered. "Have you tried the pizza at Enzo's?" he asked, the corners of his mouth struggling to smile.

I sat on the edge of the bed and took his hand in mine. "Enzo's is the best," I said. "But I was thinking maybe we'll go with Campbell's chicken noodle tonight? Or maybe a little vanilla ice cream?" But he had already drifted away, his breathing shallow and raspy, sleeping the sleep of the dying.

I curled into the chair beside the bed and pulled a blanket around me. I thought about Chris and her friends, women I didn't know but could call *day or night*. I wondered how it felt to be confident enough to say, *I'm in*, without knowing exactly what you were in for. And then it struck me that I'd done the same. I'd made an unspoken commitment to Neil. And he to me, in a way. We sheltered each other from unwelcome questions, from the worst parts of the world and ourselves.

---

I kept vigil through the coldest weeks of winter. The minute details of Neil's care filled my days and nights. He spent more hours asleep than awake, and I watched while he slept and searched his eyes when he woke, ready with comforting words. I offered water and teaspoonfuls of Jell-O. I read to him from his favorite poets: Thomas, Auden, and Eliot, and I grew to love them too. I rubbed his forearms and stroked his cheeks, cooed and soothed as he waited for each dose of morphine to make its way through his bloodstream.

Early one morning, just before dawn, Neil woke with a start, gasping for air. "You're okay," I said. "I'm here." I held his hands and kissed his forehead. "I'm right here."

"I'm right here," he repeated. His breathing slowed.

"That's right. We're here. Everything is okay. Have a little drink of water," I prompted, tilting the glass to his lips. "That's it."

He lifted his head and sipped. He looked at me in the dim light. "I didn't know what to do for Marcus."

Neil had not spoken of Marcus since the day I'd asked about the photograph. "I'm sure you did everything you could," I said.

"It happened so quickly. He was fine. Then he just collapsed in the street. We didn't know he was sick. We didn't know." Neil's eyes brimmed with tears.

I offered him another drink of water, and he turned his head away.

"He went to the hospital. I was with him for the first few days, then his mother came and took over. *Only one visitor*, they told us. *Next of kin.* And he never got out of hospital. He died in just a few weeks."

"I'm sorry," I said. I didn't know what else to say.

"I wish I'd done more," he said. "Wish I'd known what to do."

"You loved Marcus. I'm sure he knew. That was enough. That was everything."

Neil closed his eyes and turned onto his side, wincing with the effort. I sat on the edge of the bed and rubbed his back until I was certain he was asleep. I wasn't sure he would remember our conversation in the morning. Some days, his mind drifted as though it couldn't find a comfortable place to rest, and I did my best to ease him through these moments. I knew that even if he did remember telling me about Marcus, he wouldn't bring it up, and I wouldn't either. I knew what it took to confide in someone, to share unbearable anguish and shame. I could never ask Neil—or anyone—to go there twice.

I walked to the dresser and picked up the photo of Neil and Marcus. They looked so young, so carefree. I set the photo on Neil's nightstand. "You're not alone," I whispered. I wondered what would happen after Neil was gone, then banished the thought from my mind.

Over the next weeks, I remained methodical and composed, at least on the surface. I was hyper-focused and attentive to each solemn task. But especially in the evenings, while Neil slept, my thoughts wandered. Since the newspaper article and my conversation with Rachel, I couldn't stop thinking about things I might have done differently. I composed a litany of hypothetical questions.

*What if I had followed the rules? What if I had done the right things all the time and not just when I thought someone was watching? What if I had worn the blue gingham dress instead of the bright pink one? Kept my coat on and my buttons buttoned? Worn pants instead of a skirt? What if I had been as shiny and perfect as the gold stars on my spelling tests?*

*What if I had listened? Really listened. What if I had heeded every warning, been alert to danger in all its insidious guises? Heard not only the rumors but also the subtle cautions? What if I had pressed my ear to the door of the cloakroom, the rectory, the confessional, and heard the whispers and whimpers, the bargaining and pleading? What if I had let it all in instead of blocking it out?*

*What if I had prayed? What if I had bowed my head and prayed during mass instead of flipping through the hymnal and gnawing at my cuticles? What if I had fallen to my knees or lain prostrate, like a holy martyr? What if I had asked God about things that mattered, real life-and-death things, not just for donuts after mass and to be invisible? What if I had said the words and felt them? Could my prayers have changed everything, taken away all the bad and left only the good?*

*What if I had been brave? What if I had said something sooner, allowed words to gather in my mouth and spoken even just a phrase or two, made bold confessions no one wanted to hear? What if I had written everything in a ruled notebook, like* Harriet the Spy, *then read it aloud to anyone who would listen? What if I had told my worst secrets to someone with power, to a Superman capable of stopping a runaway train? What if I had been bold enough to pry my skinny arm from his grasp, and run away and keep running?*

*What if I had said NO? Said it and said it and said it and said it and never stopped.*

Neil died quietly. He did not utter profound last words. He did not writhe or gasp. His body lay perfectly still. His eyes did not flutter. His expression was not strained, nor was it blissful. There was no evidence that he had seen a bright light or a host of angels. He looked the same as he had for weeks. I put my hand, then my cheek to his face to try to feel his breath. I picked up his wrist, like they do in the movies, but could feel only my own throbbing pulse. I didn't call anyone. Chris was scheduled to arrive within the hour, so I waited.

I filled a basin with warm water and dampened a cloth. I wiped Neil's face and carefully eased the sleep from his eyes and the dried spittle from the corners of his mouth. I combed his hair and smoothed his pajama shirt. I washed his hands and forearms, and crossed them over his still chest, then folded the bedsheet under his chin just so. I felt I should say something. A poem, a prayer, or a sacred psalm. But words might have disrupted the subtle charge in the air, the last trace of Neil in the room. I picked up the framed photograph of Neil and Marcus I had moved to his nightstand a few weeks before. I wiped it with the tail of my shirt and ran my finger over the glass, tracing Neil's outline. Lingering dust clung to my finger.

When Chris arrived, she wrapped her arms around me, and I sobbed into her generous shoulder. She phoned the funeral home, and we waited for them to arrive and take Neil's body to the crematorium. There would be no funeral, no memorial, no further goodbye. I watched the hearse drive away while Chris stripped and remade the bed. Then she made coffee, and we sat at the kitchen table in silent grief.

Eventually, Chris spoke. "You did it," she said, as though I had accomplished something extraordinary. "You kept him out of the hospital and gave him a little bit of dignity. That's something."

It seemed like so little.

Chris reached into her bag and pulled out a large manila envelope. "This is for you," she said.

Inside were two envelopes, a letter-sized one on which Neil had written my name, and a larger one with his lawyer's business card stapled to the corner. "What is this?" I asked.

"I couldn't tell you, but Neil asked me to give it to you after he passed." Our eyes locked, and she said, "You don't have to deal with that today. Leave it until morning. Would you like me to stay? I can sleep on the couch. It might be nice to have someone in the house tonight."

"You would do that?" A wave of relief washed over me, and I began to cry again.

"Let's get you to bed." As we climbed the stairs, I leaned on Chris, my empty body heavy with loss.

---

I squinted at the clock. *11:15?* Without my glasses, I couldn't be sure. And I didn't know if it was morning or night, if I had slept a few minutes, or twelve hours, or twenty-four. I could hear the ticking of the hot water pipes and movement in the kitchen below. I smelled coffee and bacon. Chris. By the time I made my way downstairs, she had set the table and was whisking eggs.

"You're up," she said. "I was going to wake you soon. You slept a long time."

"I guess I was tired," I said, yawning.

She smiled and set a mug of black coffee on the table. "I went ahead and started breakfast. Did you even eat yesterday?"

I shrugged. "Thank you for everything. I'm not sure what I—what Neil—would have done...."

"Don't even," she said.

We ate in silence. Chris insisted on doing the dishes, then gathered her bags. "I'll check in on you tomorrow," she said.

I was used to the quiet house, but without Neil, the air was stagnant. I wandered from room to room and ended up lying on Neil's bed, staring at the ceiling. I considered packing my clothes and books, maybe taking some things home the next day after church. But the thought of sitting in a pew with my parents intensified my grief. I ached to my core. I rolled onto my side and fell into a dreamless sleep.

When I woke, long gray-blue shadows spanned the snow. I warmed leftover coffee and stared at the envelopes from Neil. I took a deep breath and opened the one with my name on it. Neil's broad cursive filled a single page.

*I am writing this letter on November 1, 1987. If you are reading this in 1988, I will have outlived the doctors' expectations, and my own.*

*Enclosed is an envelope containing the original of my will. Zara Mandela is my lawyer. Contact her to set legal processes in motion.*

*Zara will approach the brokers at the office and notify them of my intent to divide ownership of Holmes Realty among them. The ownership will be split seven ways, with the six brokers each holding a share and you holding a seventh. You may keep your share and continue to work as their office manager, or study for your license and become a broker. Or you may decide to relinquish your share, in which case the partners will buy you out. There is no hurry to decide about this. Zara will act as legal counsel to put whichever arrangement in place.*

*The remainder of my estate—the house and my savings—I have left to you. My intent is to give you the financial means to do whatever you choose—go back to school, travel, or take time to get your life together. My savings alone, invested well, will provide a good income. Do not feel you must keep the house. It holds happy memories for me, but it is just bricks and mortar. Do with it what is best for you.*

*I realize this is a lot to take in. We have known each other only a short time, but in that time, we have become closer than most. When I was diagnosed, it was a shock. I had been home for a couple of years, and I guess I thought being in a smaller city would protect me somehow. I should have let you know about my status sooner. There are so many things I left unsaid. Perhaps if I'd had more time, I would have found the words.*

*With gratitude and love,*

*Neil*

I read the letter several times, trying to make sense of it. I had not considered what would become of Holmes Realty or the house. I was overwhelmed by Neil's generosity, unable to process its implications. I put the letter back in the envelope and promised myself I would call Zara on Monday.

---

The next morning, I went to church and slid into the pew beside Rachel and my parents. The opening hymn washed over me in gentle waves. "He's gone," I whispered to Rachel. I knew she would tell my parents so I wouldn't have to.

My parents and I had a quiet understanding. We had become expert at small talk, speaking only of easy, everyday things. When I began staying with Neil, we had even less to say. Our exchanges were brief, and my parents rarely asked questions. We never, ever talked about the past. Breaching our long-standing agreement seemed cruel, and I wasn't certain how or when to break the silence. But if I didn't move home, if I stayed at Neil's house, I would have to tell the entire story, determine its beginning and end, and account for all the details in between.

The homily that Sunday was about Purgatory, which had been one of Sister's favorite topics. I remembered her telling our fifth-grade class that Purgatory is not hell but an in-between place where unworthy souls wait for God to let them into heaven. We folded our hands on our desks, and Sister led us in prayers *for the poor souls lingering in Purgatory*. We asked the saints to pray for them too, because it would take every effort to save them. A place of grayness and longing, Purgatory sounded worse than hell because of its faint promise of hope.

---

I went back to work at Holmes Realty, and in many ways, it was like I had never been away: the same paperwork, the same repetitive-yet-satisfying tasks: photocopying, stapling, filing. Even the brashest of the brokers softened as the reality of Neil's gift to them set in. They treated me like a partner, including me in conversations and inviting me for drinks on Fridays after work. We talked about Neil, which was not as difficult as I'd feared. They reminisced about Neil in the office, stylishly dressed, chatting about films and books, always interested in their lives, their children, their holidays in the Caribbean. Through our conversations, memories of Neil as I'd known him a year before began to return, reemerging gradually like a Polaroid photo from happier days. At the same time, I sensed that even those people who had worked with him for years didn't know much about Neil, about his life before he became their friendly boss. Nothing was said about his illness; if they knew he had AIDS, they didn't say, circling but never landing on the subject. I wanted to say something, to tell them about his humility and suffering and strength, about the story of Neil I had pieced together over months of caring for and learning from him. I had the words, but I could not muster the courage. I couldn't take the risk that they might judge Neil, that they would see him differently, even in death. I wondered what Neil would do, what he would say, if he had a chance to do it all again.

---

Neil's house was still and silent, fertile ground for doubt. For a while, I went to church more often, searching for answers to questions I was afraid to ask. I put on my good coat and went on Sundays and First Fridays. I stood, sat, and knelt. I prayed for people I knew and people I didn't. I prayed for strength and hope. I sang and chanted, bowed my head and asked forgiveness for my many sins. *Mea culpa, mea culpa, mea maxima culpa.* It felt the same, but also different. *Lord, I am not worthy to receive you,* I said, and finally I began to understand the dire implications of those words. No matter how much I prayed, it would never be enough.

In school, we had been taught that faith is a gift. We were told that some people are endowed with a faith that burns bright and hot and can never be extinguished. The rest of us must pray for the kind of faith that never wavers. *Look to the saints,* we were told, especially the Virgin Martyrs who were condemned in life but redeemed in death. We said special prayers to Saint Agnes, Patron Saint of Girls, who was beautiful and rich but was sentenced to death for refusing her pagan suitors. Because of her faith, Saint Agnes could work miracles, right up to the end. She was dragged through the streets naked but wore her faith like a shield. Her hair grew long to cover her body, a blessed miracle. Men who tried to rape her were struck blind, and when the authorities tried to burn her at the stake, the flames would not consume her. In the end, she was beheaded, and the devout gathered cloths and soaked up her holy blood. Agnes was twelve, which was young to have experienced so much tragedy. But unlike ordinary girls, she had the kind of faith that enabled her to rise above it all.

Several weeks after Neil died, I went to my parents and told them about his will and that I would be living in his house. They reacted with silence and furrowed brows. I wished I'd told them when Rachel was home to smooth the way. "I know it's a lot to take in," I said. "I'm still getting used to the idea myself."

After a long pause, my dad said, "This is a real opportunity for you. You'll make your own decisions, you always have. But you need to think seriously about going back to school, getting an education, making something of yourself." My mother nodded in agreement.

"Maybe you could come and see the house sometime," I offered.

My mother stood and began clearing the table. My dad said, "Don't be a stranger. We'll expect you home for Sunday dinners."

On the walk back to Neil's house, I replayed Dad's words: "We'll expect you home. . . ." In the past year, my life had changed so much. I'd always thought of my parents' house as home. But that was beginning to change too.

---

I began to make Neil's house my own. I found distractions in the work of packing up knickknacks, removing family photos from the walls, and rearranging the furniture. Chris helped me sort through Neil's clothes, and we each kept a sweater to remember him by. Chris picked a navy cashmere pullover, and I chose a hand-knit gray cardigan still bearing his scent. I also kept a few of his T-shirts, the softest ones, thin from wear. We loaded Chris's van with boxes and dropped them at Goodwill.

I spent an afternoon going through Neil's desk drawers. He had prepared for his death. Everything was in perfect order. A file labelled TAXES contained several years of past returns bound with an elastic band and his accountant's business card. He left no old receipts or ticket stubs, no diaries or love letters. But for the photo of Marcus, he left no trace of his existence before the past year, no indication that he had dreamed or travelled or loved, that he had a life before I knew him. I set aside files to be returned to the realty office and shredded anything outdated or unnecessary.

I looked around Neil's room. His bed was neatly made, as though waiting for him to turn down the sheets. His books still lined the shelves and his record collection flanked the stereo. We had spent so many hours in that room, in conversation and in crisis. I was tempted to sleep there, just one more night. But I knew it was too soon. I found a large shoebox, then collected a few items from the room—the framed photograph of Neil and Marcus, the gooseneck lamp from his nightstand, a pen and pencil set, and a dog-eared copy of *Leaves of Grass.* I closed the door behind me and went into the next room, my room, and placed the mementos on my nightstand. I sat on the bed and ran my hand over the book and the pen set in its smart leather box. I admired their simple beauty, the way they had somehow been sanctified by Neil's use. The entire house reminded me of Neil, but I wanted to have these few simple things close by, talismans for the days ahead.

---

I kept busy enough most days, but memories of Father started to prod and dig again. They did not respect time or place. Awake or asleep, at home or at work, in random idle moments, I was prey to their sinister advance. Something needed to change. I just wasn't sure what or how or when.

The phone rang one evening, just as I was getting into bed. Chris apologized for calling so late. "It's kind of an emergency. I need a favor," she said. "I have a patient I've been nursing at home for a few weeks. He lives with his parents, and when they found out he has AIDS, they threw him out. I'm trying everything I can think of to avoid the hospital, and I've run out of options. I would take him home with me, but my apartment is up three flights of stairs. Would you be okay if he stayed at your place, just for a night or two, until I can figure something out?"

"Sure," I said. "Of course. When will you be here?"

"I'm five minutes away. Thank you so much." She hung up.

I pulled on some clothes, gathered bedding from the linen closet, and ran downstairs to make up the pullout couch in the den. Part of me wondered what I had gotten myself into, but my uncertainty was overshadowed by the satisfaction that Chris had called, that she knew I would be willing to help. Just as I placed the second pillow on the bed, Chris knocked. "Hello!" she shouted. "Anybody home?"

When I entered the kitchen, she was easing a wheelchair through the back door.. "This is Curtis," Chris said.

"Good to meet you," I said. Curtis was slumped forward in the chair, and the brim of his baseball cap covered his eyes. He did not lift his head but slowly extended his hand. "Let me show you the bed I've made up." Chris gave me an encouraging nod, and I led the way to the den and helped her transfer Curtis from his chair to the bed. With his head on the pillow, I could see his face. He was young, maybe twenty-five.

"I'm sorry," Curtis said, his voice little more than a whisper. He turned his face to the wall.

"You don't need to be sorry," I said. My eyes filled and my heart ached. I knew what it was like to feel sorry for things beyond your control. What could I say to ease his pain, even a little? I looked to Chris for reassurance, then cleared my throat. "I'm glad you're here. You're more than welcome. I'll be right back with a glass of water. And how about some tea and toast?"

Chris answered for him. "That would be good, I think. I'll give you a hand."

In the kitchen, Chris took my forearm. "You have no idea how much I appreciate this. He's weak—you can see that—and I couldn't think of anywhere else to go." I filled the kettle, and Chris put two slices of bread in the toaster. Then she covered her face with her hands and took a long, deep breath. "His parents. You know, I just can't wrap my head around it. I look at that beautiful boy in there. That they could just abandon him like this! You should see their house—full of trophies and medals and photos. When he was their perfect healthy son, the star athlete, the honor student, they *idolized* him. And now? To cut him out of their lives like this? I'll never understand it!" Chris, who was always so strong, so together, looked defeated. I didn't have answers for her. All I could think about was how alone Curtis must feel and how vulnerable to be entirely reliant on Chris, someone he barely knew.

Just as I was about to speak, the blackened toast popped up and smoke billowed out of the toaster. I rushed to open a window. Chris tossed the toast in the sink, then threw her arms in the air. "And now he's stuck with us—and we can't even make toast!"

I started to laugh, and Chris choked on her laughter and tears. We managed to pull ourselves together, brought Curtis his tray, and sat with him until he drifted off. "Come on," I said. "The spare bedroom has fresh sheets. Let's get some sleep."

I laid awake for a long time. I thought about Curtis's parents. Curtis's *I'm sorry* would never reach their ears—and even if it did, it served no purpose. He wore sorrow like a heavy shroud woven of injury, self-blame, and despair. I knew all too well how those three threads might become so entwined, they could never be untangled one from the other.

The next morning, I woke early. I could hear Chris snoring as I crept down the stairs. I checked on Curtis, then went to the living room. Neil's parents had called it *the parlor* and kept it *for company*. It was the one area of the house that neither he nor I had changed. Formal furniture surrounded a low walnut table on which sat a stack of oversized coffee table books: *Ancient Egypt, The City at Night, Birds of the Amazon, Georgia O'Keeffe*, and, on top, *The Sistine Chapel*. I lifted the heavy cover of *The Sistine Chapel* and removed the newspaper article about Father, pressed and yellow, like an autumn leaf.

I knelt at the table. I had read the article dozens of times, and the ink was smudged in spots. I scanned it again, pausing at each implausible number: *Eight girls…at two schools…between 1970 and 1985…six-month investigation…eight counts of indecent assault….*

But what I really wanted to read one more time was the final paragraph: *When asked about the charges, the Diocese issued the following statement: "This is, to the best of our knowledge, the first time such accusations have been waged against Father ___. The Diocese will cooperate fully with the legal process. We pray for justice and healing in these communities."*

But they *did* know. They knew because my parents and I told the Bishop. They knew because I described the most shameful moments of my life. They knew because Father's name was said ten, twenty, fifty times that day, and the Bishop said Father would no longer be in our parish. They knew because my parents signed an agreement with the Diocese to put the matter to rest, to put it behind us.

After breakfast, after Curtis was settled in front of the television and Chris went to work, I called Neil's lawyer, Zara, and told her about the charges against Father. "I know you're not that kind of lawyer," I said. "But could you contact the prosecutor in charge of the case? I have some information I want to share and I'm not sure how."

"I can do that for you. Definitely. Give me a day or two," Zara said.

When we hung up, I wiped my damp palms on my jeans and phoned my parents. My mother answered. "I'm sorry," I began. "But we have to talk." I didn't let her speak. I told her in as few words as I could that I was going to be involved with the case against Father, that I was going to tell my story. When I finished, the line was silent.

"If you think that's best," she said and hung up.

My stomach lurched with fear and regret. As I hung up the phone, I stared at the scar on my hand. The burn had healed quickly, but it had left an ugly reminder. I wandered around the quiet house. I wiped futile tears from my face and blew my nose. At the very least, she could have said, *I understand.* But how could she? The scars were mine and mine alone.

---

I stopped going to mass. On Sundays, I laid in bed, drinking coffee and reading the weekend papers. I half-watched smarmy televangelists or listened to CBC radio. I cleaned the house, did laundry, mowed the lawn. I roasted a chicken for dinner and baked banana bread. I did what other people do on Sundays.

And yet, I missed the Sunday morning rituals, sitting quietly in a pew next to Rachel and being swept up in the swell of the choir. I missed being surrounded by incense and warm bodies, easy answers and comfortable prayers. I missed greasy diner breakfasts with my family after mass. I used to feel sorry for people who didn't have these things, who were left out. I missed the smug piety of belonging.

I knew other parishioners judged me for leaving. I read into every look, every looking away. I avoided my parents and their friends. In the grocery store, I felt people staring. I gripped the shopping cart with slick palms and rushed through my list, forgot the milk or the eggs, and then had to go back, which was the last thing I wanted to do.

When Rachel phoned to tell me my parents were hosting a party for their twenty-fifth wedding anniversary, I felt a pang of guilt. I'd been avoiding them for weeks, allowing my work at the office and helping Chris care for Curtis to fill every waking hour. My mother's terse response to my decision to file an official complaint against Father still rankled, but I shouldn't have expected anything different. I especially regretted not spending enough time with Rachel. I asked her if there was anything I could do to help with the party.

"Please, just come," she said. "Next Saturday, seven o'clock." I couldn't say no to her.

When I arrived, the party was underway. I stood on the sidewalk in front of the house and watched guests mingling in the brightly lit living room. I let myself in through the back door and found Rachel in the kitchen refilling the punch bowl.

She hugged me tightly. "You came!"

"I said I would. Who are all these people?"

Rachel laughed. "You know, mostly neighbors. Some people from Dad's work. Can you help me bring food to the dining room?"

Rachel and I wove our way through the crowded house, balancing trays of hors d'oeuvres and smiling and nodding at our parents' friends.

When we reached the dining room, a family friend was holding court. "Did you see that story in the paper a while back? Those women, making a big deal about something that happened years ago, jumping on the bandwagon, just looking for attention. What's in the past is in the past. They'll bankrupt the Church with lawsuits. They need to let it go. There's no real proof of what they say." I opened my mouth but was so stunned I could not speak. I looked around at my parents' friends, some of whom I had known since I was small. Some nodded at his words, some drifted away. I wondered if my red-faced silence implied agreement or exposed me as a victim. I retreated to the kitchen, poured a few glugs of wine into a plastic cup, and sat on the little step stool in the far corner of the room.

Rachel rushed in and crouched beside me. "Are you okay?"

I shook my head. "I feel like a stranger sometimes, you know?"

Rachel put her arm around my shoulders and nodded.

"I've been wanting to tell you. I, um…I'm going to give a statement to a lawyer. About Father."

"But you…."

"You don't need to say anything. I want to do this. I need to."

Rachel nodded, blinking back tears.

Then our mom called from the doorway. "Girls! It's almost time for the toast. Come to the living room and bring the champagne."

Rachel stood, extended her hand, and pulled me up. "Let's go in there," I said.

"Are you sure?"

"Yeah," I said. "I'm sure."

---

The prosecutor called to set up an appointment for an interview. "We have a lot of depositions to conduct, more than we thought, so it's going to be a while before we get to you." Setting that date was like lighting a slow-burning fuse, like pulling the pin of a grenade and standing stark still for weeks so as not to trigger its detonation.

When the day of the interview arrived, I was interrogated like a suspect in a 1940s spy thriller, sitting at a wooden table, bright lights in my eyes. *How old were you when it happened? Five? Six? Six-and-a-half? Ten? Thirteen? Where? What time was it? Did you write it down? Did anyone see? Weren't your classmates in the next room? Wouldn't they have heard? What were you wearing? A dress? Pants? Were all your buttons buttoned, your zippers zipped? What did he say? What did you say? Did you say no? Did he give you gifts? Treats? Why did you take them? Did it happen more than once? Twice? More? Why did you stay? Why did you go back? Didn't it seem wrong to go back? How many times? Did he touch you here? There? Did it hurt? Why didn't you say so? Why didn't you leave? Had anything like this happened to you before? So you knew what was happening? If it happened the way you describe, wouldn't there have been marks? Bruises? Blood? Wouldn't someone have noticed? Wouldn't your mother have known? Did you tell anyone? Your parents? Your teacher? Why didn't you say something? You had plenty of opportunities to tell before now. Did anyone ever ask you about it? Why did you lie? That was a long time ago—are you sure you are remembering correctly? Sometimes we think we remember, but our minds play tricks on us. Why did you keep this a secret for so long?*

I answered each question. And then I answered the same questions again. And again. *Did I say four times or five? Maybe it was five times. Maybe six. Five for sure. For sure it happened five times. Five.* I second-guessed until I couldn't remember my original answers, and they said, *You are wasting our time.* I started to hear the answers in my sleep. I repeated the answers to myself on the bus, while making dinner, and lying awake in bed.

Self-doubt overtook reason. I wondered if the lawyers were right when they said there might not be enough evidence to pursue a case.

---

Nothing out of the ordinary happened in the days after I gave my statement, but the gravity of it weighed on me. I was grateful for Chris's presence in the house, and helping her care for Curtis gave me purpose. He lived at Neil's house for almost four months. He had days when his fever made him incoherent and he fought invisible demons, and days when he was too tired to fight. When his death seemed imminent, when breathing took all his energy and he no longer stirred and barely made a sound, Chris began sleeping in an armchair next to his bed so he wouldn't be alone. He died on a Wednesday morning at sunrise. Chris woke me, and we went through the now familiar tasks of calling the funeral home and saying goodbye. Chris phoned his parents, a task I knew she dreaded.

Later that morning over coffee, Chris said, "I hate that I'm getting used to this. With each new patient I think, *Please let this one have an easier time.* But they never do. It's starting to seem normal."

"You do everything you can," I told her.

"Yeah, well, this is my job. You're the one who went above and beyond," she said.

"I'm glad I could do it. If I'm honest, I think it helped me too. I haven't been myself since Neil died." I turned away and set my mug in the sink. Part of me wanted to tell Chris about making the statement, about the case against Father, but I wasn't ready. Not yet. "There's just so much space in this house," I said. "Anytime someone needs it...."

"Do you really mean that?" Chris asked. "Because if you do.... God, there are a lot of patients who need a place to stay."

We stared at each other in silence, gripped by the realization of what Neil's house could become.

# [PART 3]

Everyday things break down. Newspapers turn yellow and brittle, elastic bands dry up and snap, pencil erasers harden, clothing becomes holey from wear and moths. Even those things we cherish and take meticulous care to preserve fall apart eventually: old love letters, favorite books, heirloom furniture, marriages. All organisms disintegrate, release their fluids, decompose, return to the soil. I found an apricot behind the fridge once, shrivelled to a scrap of brown leather. *Remember that you are dust and to dust you shall return.* You, me, the apricot: just dust in the end.

It's hidden, dangerous things that hold up: shards of glass, leaky car batteries, weapons-grade uranium. They are here forever, no matter how deep we bury them. Traces of strontium-90, radioactive fallout from nuclear testing, are detectable in human baby teeth. We are bound to hazardous chemicals, and them to us, in a tenuous treaty of coexistence. There is no way to break those toxic bonds.

The word *religion* comes from the Latin *ligare*, to bind. Sacred bonds are always the strongest. The Binding of Isaac put

Abraham to the test then raised him to greatness in the eyes of the faithful. Abraham tied his son with thick rope, snugged tight-tight, an animal trussed for holy sacrifice. He checked each knot at wrists and ankles, bound Isaac to the altar, and sharpened a blade. Abraham didn't hesitate or waver; it never crossed his mind to cut the boy free. When God gave Abraham the go-ahead to release Isaac, it was on a whim, or so it seemed. Abraham became the Great Patriarch, the Father of All Nations. The deep scars on Isaac's skin were collateral damage.

We are all bound, one way or another, some of us more tightly than others. For centuries, upper-class Chinese families bound their daughters' feet, breaking the tiny phalanges, bending the toes under, then wrapping them in gauze. Ornately embroidered slippers covered all manner of wickedness: grotesque deformity, infection, necrosis. Perfumed bindings masked the stench of death. The contorted foot was considered beautiful, erotic even—the smaller the better. A tiny lotus foot could ensure marriage into a wealthy family, binding a hobbled woman *'til death do us part.*

We are bound by common law, by sacred book, by hook, or by crook. By treaties and accords, penned in ink and signed in blood. Binding agreements conceal the most heinous human acts. Some things are undoable.

# [1988–1990]

The Crown Attorney phoned and asked me to draft a written statement to read at the hearing. "Be sure to write in the first person," he said. "Tell *your* story. Try not to editorialize."

"If I do this, how long should it be?" I asked.

He asked how many words I thought I might need.

"There are not enough words," I said.

He suggested ten thousand. "That should be plenty," he added and hung up.

Ten thousand words. In the Bible, the story of Job, the very embodiment of suffering, is afforded an entire book, 12,674 words, to be precise. Dinah, raped then used as a pawn in a shady trade deal, is silent. Of course, Job had a lot to tell, not only about suffering but about atonement and redemption. His tortured laments and fraught dialogue with God warranted pages and pages. Dinah, on the other hand, was victim through and through, from start to finish.

For years, I had worn silence like a second skin. In silence I could plunge deep, deep down, like a diver in a diving bell beneath the briny chop, beyond the reach of fear and doubt. And yet, each time I reread the newspaper article about Father, I came a little closer to seeing my story as a shared story, and I knew the fate of us all rested on its telling. The story was no longer mine alone. I was beginning to understand the way my story lived both in my body and outside it. When I had first spoken to the lawyers, their questions gutted me like a knife, left me splayed and exposed. And now, if I wrote the formal statement and it was used in court, it would go *on the record* and outlast us all.

I sat on the sofa with a notepad and pen, unsure where to start. I argued with myself. *Tell the truth. The facts. Just begin.* But I didn't feel safe committing words to the page.

*Safe* is such a relative term. People stand on crowded subway platforms every day, reading books or daydreaming, fully confident they will not be shoved onto the tracks. But why shouldn't that happen? Less likely than being pushed is the probability of being rescued. What sort of person jumps onto the tracks just to be a hero?

I spent long afternoons staring at the page. I wrote and scratched out, wrote and scratched out, then tore the paper into tiny shreds. The uneven, ugly fragments of my story refused to sit quietly on tidy, blue lines.

Finally, one sunny afternoon, I made some progress. One paragraph, then another.

"What are you working on?" Chris asked.

"Oh God, you scared me!" I fumbled with my notepad, and my pen fell to the floor. I'd forgotten Chris was coming by to talk about a patient who might need a place to stay.

"Sorry," she said. "I knocked. I thought you heard me come in." She picked the article about Father up off the coffee table. "What's this?"

"It's nothing," I said, trying to steady my voice. "It's just.... It's about that trial...that priest from the church downtown."

Chris sat down beside me. "I've been wondering for a while now, but I wasn't sure if I should ask. Are you one of the victims?"

Her question caught me off guard. I almost said no. I lowered my eyes, and unbidden, the truth slipped out. "Yes," I whispered. "I.... Yes."

"I wondered," she said. "I'm sorry. There are so many of you, so many women, all your age, or a little older or younger."

"How did you know?" I asked.

"This article. I noticed it around the house—on the kitchen counter, the coffee table. Are you okay?"

I was relieved by Chris's concern. She asked without judgment or blame. We had been through so much together with Neil and with Curtis, and I trusted her more than anyone. But I wasn't prepared, and I didn't know how to answer her questions.

"There's a support group, maybe you've heard of it? CASA, it's called. Clergy Abuse Survivors' something-or-other? I think they meet at the community center. I know a couple people who are involved. It might be good for you."

"Maybe," I said. "Yeah, maybe."

---

I submitted my statement. As the trial date drew closer, I threw myself into the project of transforming the house. Chris and I spent evenings talking about what we might need to do to accommodate patients with HIV-AIDS, then consulted with a contractor about how to renovate the main floor. We met with the women who had been helping Chris, and they were astounded by our proposal: Chris and I would live full-time at the house, and with the help of volunteer nurses and caregivers, we would be able to offer three palliative care beds. This would save vulnerable gay men from the indignity of hospital care and give them a place that felt like home—or as close to home as we could make it. Chris would keep her nursing job, and volunteers would work on a rotating schedule.

Chris gave up her apartment and moved into one of the empty bedrooms upstairs, a room large enough for two. Her partner, Mila, spent several months of the year on tour as manager of a band, so she would also make her home at Neil's house. I sold my shares of Holmes Realty to the brokers and put the proceeds toward renovations. We expanded the powder room into an accessible full bath and partitioned the large family room into two bedrooms; the den would serve as the third. We added a bank of cabinets along one wall of the kitchen, including a locked cupboard for medications. Chris scrounged furniture and equipment, and before long, the rooms were ready.

One evening in late September, Chris and I hosted ten women at the grand opening of Neil's House. We sat around the dining room table and ate kebabs, Greek salad, and baklava, and drank goblets of red wine. Rachel came too, and I watched her mingle with Chris's friends. She seemed completely at ease, chatting and laughing with Sara, a volunteer who was a nursing student at the college. The room seemed to pulse and glow. The energy generated from our shared purpose was unlike anything I had ever experienced. I sat back and felt the warmth of candlelight and wine on my cheeks. When Chris quieted the group to make a toast, my eyes filled with happy tears. "To Neil and Neil's House," Chris said, raising her glass.

He would love this, I knew. I hoped the feeling of satisfaction and belonging would carry me through the coming weeks.

The next morning over coffee, I spotted the ad in the paper:

ARE YOU A VICTIM OF SEXUAL ABUSE BY A PRIEST?
YOU ARE NOT ALONE.
WE'RE HERE TO LISTEN.
CASA: CLERGY ABUSE SURVIVORS' ALLIANCE

Chris was right. I needed to go. As little as I wanted to talk about what happened, especially to strangers, I needed to find a way to get through the court case. I feared it would be worse than I could imagine, worse than my worst nightmares.

The following Thursday evening, after a day of stocking medical supplies for the volunteer nurses at Neil's House, I cupped a steaming mug of tea and took a seat on a metal folding chair at the community center. As we introduced ourselves around the circle, it became clear that we came from everywhere—from uptown and downtown, from the suburbs and the back roads. Some of us had spouses and children. Some of us had friends. Some of us had no one. Some of us were born with every advantage and now had university degrees, careers as physicians, professors, accountants.

Some of us had lived this for decades; some, for mere months.

I said nothing. I read the room. I listened. A woman in a green cardigan referred to herself as an RC—*a Recovering Catholic*—and everyone laughed. I could tell the laughter was disconcerting to some but comforting to others; an outsider would have found it crass. The humor surprised me, but it was a blessed relief. A woman with a furrowed brow gave an update on pending court cases. A middle-aged woman sucked her teeth in disgust. A slim man sobbed into an oversized handkerchief. Two hours later, I was exhausted, emotionally and physically. But as I left the meeting, I knew I would return. For better or worse, these were my people, the only people who could truly understand what I had been through and what was yet to come.

At my second meeting, I recognized two girls from my school. They were a grade ahead of me. I avoided their glances, embarrassed for them and myself. They sought me out at the break. We spoke in code, a sacrosanct language only we knew. *You too? You too?* We wept for the trauma we had buried and carried, for all we had lost. We extended our hands to one another and squeezed tight to still the trembling.

Week after week, we told our stories, and they accumulated like late-winter snow, deep and heavy. We assembled a litany of indictments, a breviary of abominations. I listened to every word. I nodded. *Yes, yes, yes.* Nothing could surprise me.

The sameness of our stories was jarring. We wondered at the similarities, at our shared sadness, rage, and despair. The stories overlapped like decoupage: same times and places, textures and tones. Same schools, same youth groups, same friends of friends. Same shame and denial. So many priests. And the same Father.

> *It started when I was six, and it went on for years. When I finally told my mother—I think I was about thirteen—she slapped me with all her strength. She yelled, "How could you how could you how could you how could you?" She kept hitting my face and my head with both hands until I collapsed on the floor.*

> *When I told them, my parents dragged me to the rectory. They yelled, "Tell Father what you said, you dirty girl! Tell Father what you told us!" And I just stood there crying. He told them it's not*

*uncommon for girls to say these things. That I was "mistaken," that I was "troubled." That I saw his concern as something more and created this terrible story. And my parents booked a counselling session for me with the perv. He just stood there smiling. Told my parents, "Leave her with me."*

*It went on for about two years. He did it right in our house, right under my parents' noses. And my dad was a teacher, my mom was on the school board. When I told them, I thought my parents had maybe suspected something, but they were caught totally off guard. I mean, they believed me, but it almost killed them. For the longest time, I felt bad for saying anything. Sometimes I still do.*

*My parents were so embarrassed, just mortified at the impropriety of it. They kept saying things like, "It doesn't matter how it happened. We don't need to know all the details. As long as it's stopped." They put the house up for sale two days later and we left town. We never spoke about it again.*

*I was in the church. It was a Friday afternoon, and Father picked me to help clean. You know, back then, it was a real honor to help at the church. So, I was cleaning the kneelers, wiping away the salt stains with a damp cloth. It happened so fast. He came from behind. He covered my mouth with his hand and tugged at the back of my jeans. I think he used a candlestick, forcing it in. When he was*

> *finished, there was blood, and I was crying. He threw the rag at me, the one I'd used to wipe the kneelers, and told me to clean myself up.*

The horror of each story took time to sink in. To me, the most troubling stories were those set in the Bishop's office. It seemed each of us believed we had been the only one who had met with the Bishop, held his steady gaze, trusted his assurances that he would handle everything, that he would make it right. We believed him when he said this was a shock, that no such allegations had ever been raised before. That it had all been an *unfortunate mistake*, that it *wouldn't happen again*. Some parents signed agreements—and some of us signed too. We signed to help the Bishop make it right, to seal the record. *Of course, we don't ever want your daughter's name to become public. This is a matter of the strictest confidentiality and will be kept in our sealed files.* In hindsight, we were complicit in our own persecution. It was too much to take in.

Chris insisted I call her for a ride home from CASA meetings, but I never did. Instead, I walked for hours, alone in the cool darkness. I walked along the lake, then weaved up and down side streets. Sometimes when I reached the house, I'd sit for a while on the back porch, not ready to see the volunteers or the residents or even Chris. I let my body adjust to the new layers of anger and revulsion, allowed the emotion of the evening to crystallize and settle on me like hoarfrost. When I finally went inside, the frost melted into my hair and clothing, chilling me to the bone. I ran a hot bubble bath, and my tears disappeared into the sudsy water.

Outsiders might think us naïve. Certainly our trust was misplaced, our goodwill exploited. It took many CASA meetings before I could see the big picture and begin to comprehend the awful choice we all faced: denial or martyrdom. The Holy Martyrs, the most exalted of saints, true to the end, endured scourging, whipping, flogging, starving to skin and bone, stretching on the rack, dismemberment, tossing to the lions, boiling in oil, barbecuing on hot coals, ripping apart with iron rakes, and burning at the stake. Any and all imaginable manner of torture in order to *Keep the Faith*. And those medieval horrors were just the beginning. Today's martyrs are bound and gagged by Mother Church Herself. We suffer an imposed silence to safeguard Her sanctity. A modern martyrology grows, a list so long it would be impossible to read it aloud in our lifetime.

I continued to attend weekly CASA meetings, and in between, I busied myself with the work of Neil's House. I shopped and cooked and did mountains of laundry. I charted medication regimens and logged records of the residents' care. I managed the volunteer schedule and filled in when no one else was available. Chris and her team were providing first-rate care, but we knew some people would view an AIDS hospice as a public health risk, and we were careful to avoid such scrutiny. Together, we formed a resistance, united in our covert mission. We were guerrillas, skilled in diversion and camouflage. We came and went singly, never parked more than two cars in the driveway, and when we needed a hearse, we called in the evening, never in the light of day. We ensured that Neil's House was anonymous and unassuming, the quietest house on the block. We had nothing to be ashamed of, but still, we hid in plain sight. We kept the secrets entrusted to us in order to keep our door open and ensure the safety of our residents—and ourselves.

In the first year, we cared for nine men, some for just days, others for months. Our first official resident was Andreas, an older man who spoke softly accented English. He had lost his job in a print shop when his diagnosis became known at work, and he eventually lost his apartment too. Andreas moved into the den, where he arranged his few books and photos with great care. He lived like an aged house cat, sipping warm milk and sleeping long hours, quietly biding his final days. About a month later, Luca arrived. He had been living at home with his elderly mother who could no longer manage his care. On what Luca called his high-energy days, he commandeered the kitchen and cooked delicious meals: pasta Bolognese, mushroom risotto, chicken piccata. On his low-energy days, his mother came by taxi to sit by his bed and say the rosary. After Andreas and Luca came Marty. Then Marshall and Trevor. Then Cyril, who appeared out of nowhere on a rainy night and asked to stay. Then Michael, whose partner, Dave, Chris had nursed through his final months. Chris called Michael "The Archangel," to his delight. With Michael came his cat, a beefy orange tom named Bustopher, who became a permanent resident of Neil's House.

Some of the men we cared for had families, partners, friends; many had only us. We listened to their stories—some happy-sad, some just plain sad, some tragic—entries in a pandemic-era hagiography, an anthology of flawed saints and venerable sinners yet to be written.

Chris nursed us all, through acute crises and everyday doubts. She cared for the residents as their bodies deteriorated and their spirits failed. She nursed the volunteers, myself included. She showed us how to *be* in the presence of precarious life, how to tread lightly yet confidently, gently yet surely, how to maintain calm in moments of suffering and ease tension in times of stress. Almost three decades of nursing had not dulled her sensitivity but instead sharpened her awareness of everything a nurse should be. She met each death with the solemnity of holy witness, treated each vacated body with quiet reverence. Everyone who passed through the doors of Neil's House respected her.

But Chris was no saint. She left crumbs in the butter dish and toothpaste in the sink, and she never replaced an empty toilet paper roll. She ate and drank a bit too much and was a closeted smoker, despite claiming to have quit. She was an excellent nurse but would have been a difficult patient. Her humor was self-deprecating, and she could not forgive herself for even the tiniest mistakes. She was easily frustrated when residents' families were unaccepting, and she was hard on herself when she couldn't make them see their errors in judgment.

And yet, she gave generously and unconditionally. Her motivation never seemed to wane, and I wondered how this could be, how she drew from a bottomless well of energy and compassion, day after day after day, rarely taking time for herself. I asked her once, *How do you do it?* In typical Chris fashion, she turned the tables and asked, *How do you?* When she asked such questions, they gave me pause. Chris helped me see new facets of myself, abilities and traits I didn't know I possessed.

Several months after Chris moved in, her partner, Mila, came home to Neil's House for the first time. Mila was the manager of Hot Lunch Box, an up-and-coming lesbian country-punk band, and they had just finished a long European tour. On the day she arrived, Chris, Rachel, and I spent the afternoon cleaning the house and cooking dinner. When Mila came through the door with an oversized duffel bag and an acoustic guitar slung over her shoulder, she shouted, "Hey, baby! I'm home!" and literally swept Chris off her feet.

Michael, our only resident at the time, joined us for caprese salad and pasta carbonara. Mila told stories of her travels with the band through Norway, Sweden, Denmark, the Netherlands. With her Scottish accent and cropped hair, Mila resembled Annie Lennox, which heightened her rockstar glamor. Rachel was trying to play it cool, but she hung on Mila's every word. She asked a million questions about Hot Lunch Box, and when Mila asked if she wanted tickets to their upcoming Toronto concert, Rachel squealed. "*Oh my God*, that would be fantastic! Thank you!"

"You really think Mom and Dad are going to let you go to a concert in the city?" I said. "Are you out of your mind?"

"Leave it to me," Rachel said. I knew she would get her way. She always did. Her confidence took her places I would never dare to go.

We talked long into the evening. Mila and Chris leaned into one another, Mila's arm around Chris's shoulder, Chris's hand on Mila's thigh. I had never seen Chris so happy and at ease.

When it came time to do the dishes, I pushed them all out of the kitchen. Rachel went home, Michael was exhausted and went straight to bed, and Chris set to work preparing his meds. As I tidied up, I could hear music. I peeked into Michael's room and saw Mila sitting beside his bed, strumming her guitar. She hummed softly, a Joni Mitchell ballad whose title I couldn't recall.

By the time I turned off the lights and headed upstairs, the house was quiet. I had changed into pajamas and propped myself in bed with a book when I heard Chris and Mila's muffled voices. I strained to hear their conversation. I crept barefoot into the hall outside Chris's door. I rested my forehead against the cool wall and listened to their exchange, Chris's familiar tone alternating with Mila's deeper, raspier timbre. I still couldn't make out many words, but their voices were warm and silken, like buttered caramel. Their easy banter and laughter rose and fell, until words melted into faint sighs and purrs, and then I could hear only thick breaths and the soft rhythm of skin against cotton.

I tiptoed back to my room and closed the door without a sound. I turned off the light, pulled the duvet over my head, and exhaled slowly, my body tense with unfamiliar yearning.

---

Living at Neil's House, I grew more comfortable with death. It was always painful when a resident died, but after many losses, the pain became if not less, then more manageable. Each time, I busied myself by boxing up personal belongings and readying the room for the next resident to arrive. Each time, I thought of Neil, the way tending to his most basic needs took on profound meaning. Even simple chores—changing linens, cleaning the bathroom, phoning the pharmacy—formed a somber ritual of remembrance.

I was in the midst of this ritual, preparing a room for a new resident's arrival, when I overheard Chris and Michael talking. They were in the next room, and Chris was administering Michael's evening medications.

"How is your pain today?" she asked.

"It's okay. The same. You know, until I got sick, I'd never taken anything stronger than an aspirin," Michael said.

"I remember your Dave saying the same thing," Chris said. She had been Dave's in-home nurse for six months before he died.

"Yeah. Then after he was diagnosed, he had so many drugs they wouldn't all fit in the medicine cabinet. Before you started coming to the house, I could barely keep them all straight."

"I've heard that before," Chris said. "I'm not sure how people manage on their own. You were really wonderful with Dave."

"Thanks," Michael sighed. "But I didn't always know what to do. I second-guessed myself all the time. And I did things I wasn't proud of."

Chris didn't respond. I could hear her moving around the room, wheeling the IV pole into position beside the bed, pouring a glass of water, and setting it on Michael's nightstand.

"I wanted to tell you," Michael began, his voice little more than a whisper.

I stopped making the bed and stood still so I could hear.

"It was so awful, seeing Dave sick. He had always been so strong. He was an athlete. It was just devastating. And he was so uncomfortable, in pain from head to toe. The light hurt his eyes, and he had headaches all the time. There was nothing I could do. We tried all kinds of medications. This was before we had you. He saw three different doctors, and they each prescribed different painkillers. Nothing worked. And I thought, what if it gets worse? It was already so bad. So I started putting away some pills, just a few at a time. All different kinds—T3s and all kinds of opiates and whatever else the pharmacy gave us."

"You don't have to tell me this," Chris said.

"I just—I need to. Before long I had a whole jar of pills and capsules, all different sizes and colors. I kept it in my sock drawer, way at the back, and sometimes I'd take it out and look at it. I'd hold it up to the light and look through it, like a kaleidoscope. And I wondered if I would have the guts to use them. I thought, how bad will it have to get? I imagined how I would grind a handful of pills in the coffee grinder, then stir them into a pudding cup. How I would spoon out the pudding and sweet-talk Dave into taking a bite, then two, then three. I felt sick just thinking about it, but it was a relief too, having a plan." Michael choked back sobs. "And the worst part was I didn't know if I was planning to do it for Dave, to put him out of his misery, or for me, so I wouldn't have to watch him suffer anymore."

I heard a creak as Chris sat on the edge of the bed. "Michael, it's okay. You're not the first person to think that way. Watching anyone suffer like that is terrible."

Michael continued to sob. "I didn't do it. I wanted to so many times, but I didn't."

"I know you didn't," Chris said.

Chris stayed with Michael for a long time. I finished making the bed, wiped out the nightstand and dresser, then wandered around the house. I opened the fridge and stared at the neat rows of pudding cups and tins of Ensure. I went into the living room and picked up a book, then put it down, unread. Finally, I stretched out on the couch. I tried to still my mind and relax, to breathe deeply and close my eyes, but my breath was uneven and my eyelids fluttered. I couldn't stop thinking about Michael, how torturous those final weeks were for him, and for Dave. Since Neil's death, I had been trying to focus on the good times we shared, replaying our conversations about books and food and life. Listening to Michael's story brought back memories of the times when I hadn't known how to ease Neil's pain. I had leaned on Chris then, but there was only so much anyone could do, and this compounded the injustice and indignity of living and dying with AIDS.

"Did you hear all that?" Chris was standing over me, a bottle of beer in each hand. She looked exhausted.

"I did. Poor Michael." I took the beer and sat up to make room for Chris.

"He's asleep now," Chris said. "He's had a shitty few years. And he's still got a long, hard road ahead of him, I'm afraid."

I started to ask how she knew that, how she was able to predict what would happen with Michael, but I stopped. She had seen enough to know. In six months with us, he had already outlived seven other residents.

Chris and I drank our beers in silence. I wondered about Michael. Had he always been so resilient, or had he grown stronger over time? I had always admired the kind of strength that enables people to endure through tragedy and loss, and in the past months, I had prayed for it more than once. But after hearing Michael's story, I understood that resilience is a mixed blessing: It gives us the strength to face challenges but also to keep secrets, even those that should never be kept.

I was out running errands when the Crown Attorney's office left a message on the machine. I listened, then listened again. Father had pled guilty, which meant a trial would not be necessary. The Crown Attorney wanted to meet with the victims to explain what would happen next, how the court would proceed. I wrote the date and time of the meeting on the back of a used envelope, then folded it four, six, eight times, and crammed it into the pocket of my jeans.

Later that evening, my entire body shook as I told Chris about Father's guilty plea and the meeting at the courthouse. "I don't know if I can go," I said. "All of us there together. I know a few of the others, the ones who come to CASA, but there are so many of us." All those people, all those stories. I didn't know if I could let them in.

"You do what's right for you," Chris said, squeezing my shoulder. "But if you decide to go, I'll go with you. You don't have to face this alone."

We sat quietly for a while, then Chris went up to bed. I knew I wouldn't be able to sleep. I stared at the television, but I couldn't follow the program. Every follicle, every nerve, every extremity tingled and hummed. What had I gotten myself into? I remembered what my mother always said when I balked at going to choir practice or a classmate's birthday party: *You've made a commitment.* Her words chafed, then and now.

---

No one knew how the press learned of the meeting, but when we emerged from the courthouse, they were there, waiting. Reporters and photographers lined the steps, pressing in as the forty of us squinted into the blinding light of midday. I heard the reporters shouting, their questions a roar of white noise, one with the glaring sun and the crush of the crowd. I made myself smaller and scurried past with the others.

Only Father's victims had been allowed into the meeting, so Chris had waited in the parking lot. When I reached her van, I was breathless.

"I got you," she said as she attempted to maneuver out of the crowded lot.

Protesters fanned the car with signs.

PRAY FOR HEALING

INNOCENT UNTIL PROVEN GUILTY

FALSE MEMORY IS A CONSPIRACY

WE TRUST IN FATHER

LIES! LIES! LIES!

I shielded my eyes and pulled my scarf across my mouth. I didn't dare look at the crowd for fear I would see someone from church who might recognize me.

When we got home, Chris asked about the meeting. I couldn't remember much, just that victim impact statements would be read at the sentencing and that the Crown Attorney's office would be in touch.

"Will you give a statement?" she asked.

"I don't know," I said. "I don't know if I can."

Chris nodded. "If you decide to do it, I'll be there."

I hugged her tightly. I'd known she would, even before she offered. But even with Chris's support, I couldn't imagine facing the other victims, the lawyers, the protesters, the reporters, and photographers. They all wanted pieces of me, slices of memory, and shares of truth. What would be left of me after they had their fill?

In the weeks that followed, the press blurred the line between compassion and self-interest. The victims stood united in our silence. The more we refused the reporters' requests, the more relentless they became. They sniffed and probed like drug dogs at an airport luggage carousel. They rang our doorbells and followed us to our cars. They came to the schools and factories and hospitals and offices where we worked, and they waited for us in parking lots. They tracked us at the mall and wheedled their way into checkout lines behind us. They befriended our neighbors, our yoga instructors, our therapists. They phoned our families and told them awful details of the case, horror stories our parents never wanted to hear. They folded themselves in half like looseleaf paper and slid through mail slots. They staked out churches, kneeling quietly in the last pew.

*Just a minute of your time*, they said. *Tell your side of the story.* We glared in disgust or hurried past, red-faced and perspiring. *People need to know the truth*, they pleaded. We hesitated for a split second, then slammed a car door on a steno pad or microphone. *We're on your side*, they said. *We've been working on this for years. We just need one more source, one more story. Confirmation.* But their years of asking questions had amounted to little more than a speculative feature in the Sunday paper and a few segments on the local evening news. Some stories quoted a young priest from the chancellery office. He looked so very sad, so keen to make amends. *It's unimaginable,* he said, bowing his head. Yet we could imagine it like it was yesterday, and we knew he could too. We knew what he knew, and the reporters knew, and everyone reading the paper and watching the television knew. But no one would risk saying it aloud.

There were dozens of us, dozens of same-yet-different stories, but the reporters' questions were unanswerable. I still didn't know how I was going to compose a victim impact statement that I could read in front of a courtroom full of people. I definitely couldn't bear to see my story in print, to know it would be tossed on every doorstep in the city and read over coffee and toast, along with the horoscopes and the want ads.

*Someone else would feed the vultures,* I thought. Someone else would make that sacrifice.

---

When Rachel phoned and asked me to come to the house for pizza, I was ready to say no. I hadn't seen my mother in weeks, and I didn't want to. I didn't want to know what she thought about the sentencing. I knew from our phone call that she didn't approve of, or didn't understand, me joining the court case, and the idea of hashing it out with her was just too much. But when Rachel said, "Mom and Dad are going to a party. It'll be just the two of us," I looked forward to our visit all day.

I picked up Enzo's pizza on my way, which we devoured, then we went to Rachel's room and sat on her bed, just as we had a hundred times before. "It's been so long," Rachel said.

I agreed. "I love seeing you at Neil's House. I'm so glad you've started to volunteer. But this is like old times."

And just like old times, Rachel began telling me all about her friends and school and her upcoming piano recital and swim meets. She told me about going to the Hot Lunch Box concert with Sara, the nursing student she'd met at the grand opening of Neil's House, and how much fun they'd had together. She talked with her hands and punctuated each anecdote with laughter. *We're so different*, I thought. But I couldn't have felt closer to anyone else, and as she chattered on, I was relieved that this was still true, even now that we didn't see each other often.

When Rachel went to the kitchen to make tea, I took in the little changes to her room. Her doll house and teddy bear collection were gone, replaced by a beanbag chair and bookcase, and the walls were lined with pennants from varsity volleyball, swimming medals, and honor roll certificates. She wasn't a little girl; she was almost eighteen, I reminded myself. On her desk, beside her math and physics textbooks, sat a framed photograph of the four of us: Mom, Dad, Rachel, and me. I picked it up and tried to remember when it was taken. Maybe for the parish directory, I thought. Was I ten? Eleven?

"Hey, that's a keeper, isn't it?" Rachel said as she set steaming mugs on her nightstand. "Look at our matching dresses. What was Mom thinking?"

"You were adorable," I said, putting the frame back in its place.

We drank our tea and talked for a while longer, and then I noticed the time. I wanted to leave before my parents got home. At the front door, I hugged Rachel and said, "We'll do this again soon."

"Hey, just a second," she said and ran back toward her room. She returned with the family picture. "Here," she said, pressing the frame into my hands. "You should have this."

When I got home, I set the photo on my dresser beside the

photo of Neil and Marcus. I smiled at Rachel's gap-toothed grin. My parents had hardly changed. I looked closely at myself, the way I had smiled on cue. I was so compliant, so eager to please. No one would have known what I was going through with Father, the cold dread I carried everywhere I went. I looked closer. There was something there—in my dark eyes, in the slight downward tilt of my chin. It was hard to see, but the fear was there. Why hadn't anyone noticed? Why hadn't my parents seen it? They had been conscientious about my health, my education, my appearance. Why not this? I swallowed my disappointment.

I turned my thoughts to Rachel, focused on my gratitude for her. Over the past months, I had come to admire her strength. I'd put a lot on her, telling her about Father. I didn't regret it, but it was a heavy weight for her to carry. *I should have told her about the sentencing, about the victim impact statement,* I thought. I picked up Neil's pen set from the desk and removed the sleek silver ballpoint. I took some sheets of loose-leaf paper from a drawer and began writing Rachel a long letter, an epic confession and apology, for everything revealed and hidden, said and unsaid.

---

The more I stared at our family photo, the more I understood: If you really want to know the facts, you need to know where to look. In almost every family, photographs preserve the evidence. Thousands upon thousands of images, pages and pages of glossy memories are stored in family rooms and basements, on bookcases and mantels, in scrapbooks and forgotten cardboard boxes, in damp crawl spaces and dusty attics. Folded and creased in wallets, pressed in family Bibles, and used as bookmarks. These form an archive of emotions. Dates inked on the back of snapshots, some with names, some without. Babies in lacy gowns and satin bonnets suspended over marble fonts, parents beaming. Shy girls like porcelain dolls in First Communion dresses clutching tiny purses. Confirmations and graduations, award ceremonies and golden anniversary dinners. Smiling faces, willing and unwilling subjects peer out of tarnished silver frames on desks and dressers. Some line staircases or hang in bright living rooms where they fade in the sun.

The homes of all our family friends had photos that included Father. In candid shots and group photos from all their special events, Father leans in, smiling. In some pictures he is young, clean-cut, with a boyish grin and shining eyes. But for the collar, it is difficult to tell the priest from the young dads. In other photos Father is older, with graying temples and a few laugh lines, which make his smile look a bit tight. Still, he is confident: He is the celebrant, the honored guest. He knows what young parents need: a focused gaze, a confident tone, comforting words, guidance.

If you were to compare photos of Good Catholic Families, the mothers' faces are the most varied. Some are radiant Madonnas, beaming at their children. A few direct that same adoring gaze at Father, so handsome and attentive. Some look overwhelmed, perhaps by motherhood, perhaps by the pressures of the day. If you look very closely, you can see they have tried to conceal dark circles with Pan-Cake and powder. They've been up before the sun, have agonized over which Sunday dress will best hide post-pregnancy pounds. Tables laid, folding chairs counted, they worry about the afternoon's party. *Will there be enough deviled eggs? Enough punch? Did I order a big enough cake? Will the baby go down for her nap?*

Some mothers' faces are more difficult to read, but the experienced eye can see that their smiles are forced, that they lean ever so slightly away from the group, toward the edge of the frame. Under the makeup, behind the strained smiles, they wear a here-but-not-present gaze. Some of these images look slightly blurry or overexposed, as if the mothers shuddered or blanched at Father's crocodile smile and a baby's tight grasp on his index finger.

If you look even closer, if you know exactly what to look for, you can tell that the mothers of the mothers know something. You can see it in their eyes, in the way they look at their daughters. *This will all be over soon,* they seem to say. *A glass of wine or a valium will take the edge off.*

---

The Crown Attorney phoned and left a message on the answering machine:

> *...As we explained, the judge will accept Father's guilty plea, and then he will call for victim impact statements. It's important the judge hears from as many victims as possible. This will increase our chances of a maximum sentence. We would like you to consider reading the statement you submitted to our office. If you would like help preparing to make your statement, we can put you in touch with a Victim Services advocate. Please call us back at....*

Again and again, I told myself, *I can't do it*. I couldn't imagine standing in front of a room full of people, reading those humiliating words. Again and again, I told myself I had to do it, not just for me but for all the other girls like me. I wore my indecision like a hairshirt. I writhed in sleep and thought of little else.

Wide awake at 2 a.m., I went downstairs and looked out the kitchen window at the falling snow, the first of the season. I'm not sure how long I stood there before I noticed Mila had joined me. She still had another few days with Chris before the band went back on the road.

"Hey," she whispered. "Want hot chocolate?"

"Why not," I said and filled the kettle.

We took our cocoa into the living room and sat at either end of the sofa. "I'm so tired," I said. "But I can't sleep."

"Chris told me you've got a lot going on. Do you want to talk about it?"

And I did. I told her how I didn't know what to do about the victim impact statement, how I felt sick just thinking about it. How I didn't want to give it but knew I should. And then I told her about Father and what he'd done, everything in the statement I'd written and more, every appalling detail. I told her things I'd never told anyone, incidents I'd forgotten until just that moment, dark memories I'd hidden so well I'd forgotten they were there. I talked for an hour, maybe more. I had to stop twice to catch my breath, but I pressed on. As it spilled out, my story gained momentum, and I felt I might bury us both in the avalanche of words.

Mila took in each phrase, each syllable, each pause, and her gaze never wavered. She didn't interrupt with comforting words or advice. She just listened, still and silent. When I finally finished, she said, "You don't know me very well yet. It means a lot that you trusted me with this."

I stared into my cup and felt a twinge of regret. "I don't know why I told you all that. I mean, I've told Chris some of it, and Rachel knows a little."

"Sometimes it's easier to talk to people you know less well. Like a therapist. Not that I'm a therapist."

"What do you think I should do?" I asked her.

"You know, I don't feel right telling you what to do. But I do know this: Sometimes, when someone takes something from you, something you can never get back, the only claim you have on it is your memory. So, when you put words to the page, and when you say them out loud, as hard as that is, it can remind you of your power. You feel weak right now. And I can't promise you that giving your statement will make everything better. But drawing on that power might help you to move on, maybe even give you strength, if that makes sense."

Mila stood and walked to the window just as a snowplow passed, its blue lights flooding the living room. "My stepdad was a right bastard," she said. "He spent half his life in the pub, and when he came home, he beat my mum and knocked me and my brothers around too. I could take the beatings. I guess I got used to them, as odd as that sounds, and when I got older, I learned to dodge him. But it wasn't until I started writing songs and poured all that sadness and hurt and anger into the lyrics that I let go of my fear. I know it's not the same thing—what you're facing is a lot bigger and a lot harder. But if what I've told you can help, even a little...." Mila turned to face me.

"Thank you," I said.

"Anything you need, my friend," she replied.

We set our mugs in the sink, and I went back to bed, exhausted by the telling.

---

The next morning, I woke to the sound of Bustopher sneezing. "Hey, buddy," I whispered. "What are you doing in here?" Of course, I knew the answer: He had figured out weeks before how to push at my bedroom door until the latch gave way, and he often came in looking for attention. "Let's get you some breakfast," I said as I pulled my robe on and slid into my slippers.

In the kitchen, Chris was filling a thermos with coffee. "Any left for me?" I asked.

"You bet," she replied and poured me a cup. "By the way, have you noticed Bustopher sneezing a lot lately?" Just then,

Bustopher sneezed three times. "Like that," Chris said, pointing. "Do you think we should take him to the vet?"

"I'll ask Michael what he thinks. But sure, I can take him."

Bustopher snorted and left the room.

I phoned the veterinary clinic around the corner and booked an appointment for later that afternoon. I found a wooden crate in the basement and lined it with an old blanket. Bustopher hopped right in, content to ride in the makeshift carrier. When I placed him on the vet's examining table, he sniffed the surface for a few minutes, sneezed, and laid down.

The vet came in and extended his hand. "I'm Dr. Hennessy. This must be Bustopher."

I explained he'd been sneezing a lot the past few days.

"Well, let's take a look." While Dr. Hennessy checked his ears and teeth and listened to his heart, Bustopher sniffed and purred. "How old is Bustopher?"

"We're not exactly sure. He was a stray. Michael, his owner, thinks around five?"

"That sounds about right," Dr. Hennessy said. "He's in good shape, and he has a nice, healthy coat. His eyes are a bit runny. And he's been sneezing?"

As if on cue, Bustopher sneezed, then scratched his left ear.

"Okay then, fella. That's quite a sneeze," Dr. Hennessy said. "I don't hear any congestion in his lungs, and his heart sounds strong. I think the issue is some sort of upper respiratory irritant. He may have allergies to something in your home, like dust or pollen, but it's more likely he's reacting to something in his diet. What are you feeding him?"

"Well, kibble from the grocery store, mostly. I just buy whatever's on sale. He'll eat anything."

"Does he eat people food?"

"He loves yogurt. And ice cream. And Cheezies and Pringles. Snack foods in general. I suppose that's not good?" I asked sheepishly.

"Not really," Dr. Hennessy said. "And a diet too high in dairy might be causing the irritation. I'm going to send you home with some samples of food that's dairy- and grain-free. Before we try anything else, let's see if changing his diet—and eliminating those snacks—makes a difference." Dr. Hennessy opened Bustopher's file. "So, when you called in, you gave the receptionist your address, and you were in our file already, under Holmes? Did you buy the house from them? Mrs. Holmes was such a nice lady. She had a little wire-haired terrier."

"That's probably right. I didn't know her."

"Did you know Neil? Her son? He and I went to high school together, if I have the right family."

"Neil was my friend," I said. "He died almost two years ago."

"I heard that. I'm sorry," Dr. Hennessy replied. "I ran into him a few times when he was running the realty office.... I'm starting to put two and two together—you must be one of the nurses at Neil's House."

I'd become expert at keeping Neil's House a secret, so to be asked about it so casually made my pulse quicken. "Well, um, I'm not a nurse, but.... How do you know about Neil's House?"

"I know Chris. Well, I know of her. Everyone in the gay and lesbian community knows Chris. People have been talking. It's wonderful, what you're doing."

"I didn't know anyone knew, just the residents and a few others. But, thanks. It's what Neil would have wanted."

"No doubt," Dr. Hennessy said. "Call me Kurt, by the way. I wonder, would you and Chris consider coming to a Gay and Lesbian Association meeting sometime to talk about Neil's House? I know people would like to know more and would want to help. You can talk to Chris about it and get back to me, if you want."

I wasn't sure what to say. It was unnerving to think people were talking about Neil's House. "I'll mention it to Chris," I said.

"No pressure. I get wanting to be anonymous. And I wouldn't dream of outing the project. But there's just so much need out there, and what you're doing—it's remarkable, really. Oh, and there's no charge for today's visit. It's the least I can do."

---

When I arrived home with Bustopher, Chris met me at the door. "We have a new resident," she said. "I would have given you a heads-up, but he needed to move right away. I set him up in the den."

"Sure," I said. "What's his name?"

"Well, here's the thing. He's kind of famous. It's Montrose Jackson."

"The writer? You're kidding!" I'd read all his novels, most of them dark mysteries. A few had been made into movies.

"He's one of my home-visit clients, and he's in a bind. He can't manage on his own right now, but we've had a hard time arranging full-time care. He doesn't want any publicity, if we can help it," Chris said. "I told him we were pretty much operating under the radar."

"Sure, of course," I said. *Montrose Jackson, in our house.* I was in awe.

"I don't think he'll be here long. He seems to be responding to a new drug cocktail. He's getting stronger, so he should be able to move home at some point."

I put the conversation I'd planned to have with Chris on hold. Kurt would understand, and in the meantime, I had to trust he would keep quiet about Neil's House.

---

About a week before the court date, Rachel showed up and insisted we go shopping.

"You know I hate shopping," I argued.

As always, Rachel persisted. "But you have to buy some new clothes. Have you looked in the mirror lately?"

I hadn't. As a rule, I avoided mirrors. It was an old habit, and one I was comfortable with.

Rachel eyed me up and down. "You haven't bought clothes in years. Everything you own is at least two sizes too big. And you can't keep wearing those gross old sweatpants."

"I washed them yesterday," I said defensively.

Rachel rolled her eyes.

"Why don't you just go pick out some jeans for me? I'll give you my credit card." I knew Rachel would say no, but I had to try.

"You need to try things on. We'll have a sisters' shopping trip. It'll be fun!"

I grumbled some more, then put on my coat. I could never say no to Rachel.

I had forgotten how the mall glittered and sparkled in December, how it felt to be jostled by cheery holiday shoppers, to be seduced by the scents of pine trees and Cinnabon. Rachel pushed through the crowds and commandeered a fitting room. "Stay here," she said. She brought armloads of clothes—jeans and sweaters, pants and blouses.

"Are you kidding me, Rachel?" I said when I noticed the size on the tags.

"Try them on," she said. "You're no bigger than me."

And she was right. Every item fit. I stood in front of a trifold mirror, staring at a person I hardly recognized. We left the mall laden with bags.

That evening, I removed the tags from my new clothes. I paired the tops and bottoms to create several matching outfits, some casual, others a bit dressier. Laid out on the bed, they looked like headless fashion dolls, thin and pretty. Nothing like me.

These were clothes for someone who went to work every day, went to concerts with her friends, went on dates. I hung them in my closet, out of sight. But after I brushed my teeth and put on my pajamas, I opened the closet and ran my hands over the silky blouses, plush sweaters, and soft wool slacks. I allowed myself, just for a moment, to remember that they were mine, that they fit as though they were tailor made for me, that I could put them on anytime I wanted to. I knew it was silly, but there was a strange satisfaction in thinking about wearing them, like I might one day put on that pale blue pullover, those Guess jeans, and be a different person.

---

I put off looking at my victim impact statement until a few days before I was to give it. I should have contacted Victim Services for help, but I had put it off too long. I dreaded reading it again, even to myself, but I knew I needed to prepare. I sat on the edge of my bed and read it silently, start to finish. Once. Twice. A third time. Then I read it aloud, very slowly, then more quickly. I practiced it word by word, phrase by phrase, the way I had practiced the clarinet when I was a girl, note by note, measure by measure, for hours on end. I memorized sentence after sentence, then paragraph after paragraph. I whispered it whenever I was alone, as I folded laundry and cooked dinner. When I recited it in the shower, it took on the sonorous tone of Gregorian chant. Some words infused the steam and dripped down the glass door; others swirled down the drain with soap suds and dead skin cells. I heard my own voice in my head, the same nine paragraphs, the same 1,824 words, over and over and over again. I practiced my statement until the words were just words, until sound had all but overtaken meaning, until each alliteration, each syllable, each digraph, each sibilant consonant lingered in my ear, the phonetic fragments a thin distraction from the horrible truths therein.

My self-imposed rehearsal schedule was exhausting. I recited the statement in my sleep, but in those dreams, I could never get to the end. I woke up each morning in a cold sweat. Then, I got up and began practicing again. I counted down the hours until I would read it in court. I feared I would lose my nerve.

---

On the morning of the court date, I woke early. I showered, then surveyed the new clothes in my closet, none of which I'd worn. I chose a pair of wool dress pants, a pale pink pinstriped blouse, and a navy cardigan with pearl buttons. I dressed, then brushed my hair to the side and clipped it in place with a wide gold barrette. I stood in front of the mirror and stared at a girl—a woman—I hardly recognized. I took off my cardigan and blouse and put on one of Neil's old white undershirts. The soft cotton against my skin was a small comfort.

I dressed again, then picked up the file folder from my nightstand. I had rehearsed my statement hundreds of times. I knew it start to finish, forward and backward, each pause and inflection, each stinging word. I was as ready as I could be.

We were standing near the back door, buttoning our coats to head out, when Chris grasped me firmly by the shoulders. "Remember to look at me and you'll be fine," she said.

I nodded and looked down at my boots.

"Chin up," she said, cupping my face in her warm hand. "You can do this. I know you can."

I looked Chris in the eye, grateful for her confidence though I knew it was misplaced. She wiped a tear from my cheek with her thumb, and we left for the courthouse.

This time, I wasn't surprised to see media vans lining the street and the throng of reporters on the steps. We hurried past them, showed our identification at the door, and made our way to Courtroom A. The press gallery buzzed with activity, and the general seating was full. A court officer directed us to the section reserved for women giving victim impact statements.

Rachel hurried toward us and gave me a quick hug. "You're here. I was starting to worry."

"Sorry," I replied. Just then, I noticed my parents across the room. I didn't know what to think. I stared at them, but they didn't notice me. My dad was reading a pamphlet, and my mother was talking to the woman seated next to her. "I can't believe they're here. I mean, they didn't say anything, and I thought...."

"They insisted," Rachel said. "I didn't think they would come. They didn't say anything to me, but they were ready to go when I was leaving the house. It'll be okay."

Chris and Rachel were talking, but I was so distracted by my parents' presence that I couldn't follow their exchange. I hadn't spoken to my mother or my dad about the trial. I had kept myself at arm's length, pushed them to the periphery of my life, and they seemed content with the arrangement. Did they know what they were in for? Would they understand? Would they believe me? There were details in my statement I hadn't shared when we met with the Bishop, horrible acts I didn't even have words for at the time.

"Hey," Chris said, placing her hand on my elbow. "Rachel's right. It's going to be okay. Just take this one thing at a time. We'll sit and listen, then you will give your statement. Everything else can wait."

I knew she was right. I gave Rachel another quick hug, and Chris and I took our seats. Beside me sat Elise, a woman I knew from CASA. She stared straight ahead but took my hand and gripped it tightly.

The judge entered, and the courtroom fell quiet. He introduced himself and explained the order of events: Father would respond to each charge, then victim impact statements would be read.

I couldn't see Father, but I knew he was across the aisle at the front of the room. I tensed at the thought of his close proximity, the same way I had as a child. My breath quickened. I looked for the exit, then forced myself to look at Chris, then at the other women victims surrounding me. *You're safe*, I thought and willed myself to believe it.

A court official read the long list of charges: *You are charged with thirty-eight counts of sexual assault of a minor, how do you plead?... Two counts of forcible confinement, how do you plead?... Two counts of aggravated sexual assault of a minor, how do you plead?... Two counts of rape in the first degree, how do you plead?*

I shuddered as each word pierced deep inside my ears. I closed my eyes and tried to block out the voices. Father's voice. *Guilty.... Guilty.... Guilty....*

I told myself: *It's okay. I'm okay.*

*I'm okay I'm okay I'm okay I'm okay I'm okay I'm okay I'm okay I'm okay.* My head throbbed with each syllable.

The court recessed, and some of the women seated in our section hurried from the courtroom, leaving wads of soggy tissue beneath their chairs. Chris asked if I needed water or if I wanted to get some air. I shook my head. We stayed in our chairs and waited. I knew if I left the room, I wouldn't come back in.

Women took the stand. One, two, three, more, their stories intersecting and overlapping. When the court officer finally called my name, I walked quickly to the dais. I kept my head down and my eyes lowered. *This is it*, I thought.

Everyone would hear my story. I would tell everyone how the abuse started when I was six and ended when I was thirteen. How it happened everywhere: at home, at church, at school. How, still today, I try to outrun those terrible memories.

I leaned into the microphone and began.

I read the story, even and measured, just as I'd practiced it.

But as I spoke, my voice flew to the far corners of the room and bounced off every hard surface: every table, wall, window, molding, and cornice. It gathered in the domed ceiling, ricocheted high in the windowed cupola, then fell like hail on the people below. Sentences hit sharp corners and fractured into words and phrases.

I heard this:

*six years old*

*Father*

*friendofthefamily like an uncle to us*

*family dinners tucked me in*

*a good girl his special helper*
*at school*
*the rectory*
*his office*
*my bedroom*

*Yes, Father.*

*no place was safe.*
*no place was safe.*

*hands on my back*
*under my clothes*
*held me down*
*pressedagainstme*
*dirty*
*silent*
*I thought I thought*

*"Our Little Secret"*
*"Be a Good Girl"*

*again and again*
*weekafterweekafterweek for years*

*until I was twelve*
*paralyzed alone*

*couldn't won't understand*
*theshameofit*
*told my parents told the Bishop*

*make it go away*

*the nightmares never the same*
*worstofall*

I was near the end—*almost finished, almost there*—when I saw movement out of the corner of my eye. Or a slight shift in the light. Whatever it was, I looked up and to the right and saw Father. I froze. I knew I should keep reading from my papers. Look at Chris. Take a breath. But I could do none of those things. I watched Father reach into his jacket pocket and pull out a candy, unwrap it, and pop it into his mouth. Watched as he crumpled the wrapper and put it back in his pocket, checked his watch, adjusted the cuff of his shirt. Watched as he removed a bright white handkerchief and wiped his glasses, holding them up to the light to check his work. Watched as he leaned back in his chair, crossed his legs, smoothed his trousers. He brushed at the sleeve of his coat, preening like a large black cat, vain and self-absorbed.

"Miss, if you're through. . . ." The court officer extended his arm.

I didn't move.

"Thank you for your statement," the judge said. "You may take your seat."

I returned to my seat, shaken and short of breath.

"You were great," said Chris. "Perfect."

"But I didn't finish," I whispered.

"No one could tell," Chris replied. She wrapped her arm around my shoulders and pulled me close. "You're so brave."

I didn't know how to respond. I didn't feel brave. But I didn't feel weak either. Seeing Father was disturbing and disorienting, but I hadn't collapsed, hadn't dissolved, hadn't shattered into a thousand pieces. It was okay that I hadn't finished. I'd said what I needed to say for the judge to consider his sentencing.

"Can we go?" I asked.

Chris gathered our coats and ushered me out of the courtroom. We rode home in silence. I thought about my parents, hearing it all a second time. I thought about Father, how he just sat there, so smug and oblivious. Had he heard me? Or any of the women who gave statements? Had he even meant it when he uttered those forty pleas? *Guilty. Guilty. Guilty.*

I thought I would feel relieved, but I just felt numb. When we got home, Chris insisted I eat something. She warmed a bowl of stew, which smelled and tasted of nothing. I went to bed and fell into a heavy, dreamless sleep.

When I woke, I felt groggy but a little lighter. I went downstairs to brew a pot of coffee and found Montrose Jackson sitting at the kitchen table surrounded by stacks of books, loose papers, pens, and pencil shavings. In the headshot on his book jackets, he was round-faced and broad-shouldered, but in person, in an oversized cardigan and plaid scarf, he was so small, a graying husk of a man hunched over a yellow legal pad, wringing his hands.

I cleared my throat. "Good morning."

He looked up, startled. "Good morning! Chris said it would be okay if I spread out here. I can move out of your way…."

"No, you're fine there, Mr. Jackson."

"It's Monty," he said. We had met only once, earlier in the week. He had been sleeping much of the time since he'd arrived, and I'd been preoccupied.

"Monty, then. It's good to see you up. Can I make you some breakfast?"

"I could eat," he replied. "But Chris and I had porridge hours ago. It's lunchtime."

I had slept sixteen hours. "Well, no wonder I'm hungry. Why don't I make us grilled cheese sandwiches?"

While I made the sandwiches and heated a can of tomato soup, Monty continued to scribble on the notepad, pausing every few lines to rub his knuckles. "My hands aren't working like they used to," he said as I cleared a space on the table for our lunch. "The doctors say it could be the medication, and Chris agrees, but nobody seems to know for sure. This book is almost finished, but I always write my initial draft longhand, and it's been slow going. I haven't even started typing. At this rate, I'll never make my deadline."

"I'm a bit rusty, but I can type," I said.

"I couldn't ask you to do that," Monty replied. "But if you want to, I can pay. My publisher wants the manuscript by the end of January."

I was thrilled at the prospect of typing for Montrose Jackson. "We can talk about it, sure," I said, trying to hide my excitement about working for an award-winning writer.

Monty began telling me about his book. "It's different from my other novels. There is a mystery to solve, but it's really a modern allegory."

I tried to listen as he talked about genre and plot, but I was overwhelmed by the prospect of typing the manuscript. The timing couldn't have been better. I had been wondering what I would do to occupy myself until the sentencing. Working for Monty would be a better distraction than reading or watching television or doing household chores. Even hanging out with Rachel, which I loved, was only relaxing to a point; there was always a moment when I'd catch her looking at me with concern or pity. Typing a long manuscript would be the perfect way to pass the hours—the more pages, the better.

"...and that's the book in a nutshell." Monty picked up his sandwich, smiling. "Do you think you'd be interested in the job?"

---

I'd forgotten how much I loved typing. From the first day of Sister Margarite's keyboarding class, I had known it was for me. I earned good grades in my other classes, but in typing, I shone.

My entire tenth grade year, I looked forward to fourth period, the hum of the electric typewriters, the rhythmic *tap-tap-tapping* of four rows of girls, twenty-four pairs of eyes on textbooks, two hundred forty fingers striking one thousand fifty-six IBM Selectric keys. I loved the precision, the tidiness of sharp, black letters accumulating in perfect rows on a stark, white page, *tap-tap-tap-tap-tap.* Before each class, Sister Margarite sticky-tacked all the perfect assignments from the previous day to the blackboard for all to see. Some days, there were five or six papers displayed. Some days, mine was the only one, *10/10 Keep up the good work* in tidy red script on the upper-right corner. On those days, Sister Margarite winked at me as she passed through the rows, ruler in hand, looking to catch an undisciplined girl peeking at the keyboard. I was embarrassed, but also proud.

I set myself up at one end of the dining room table and typed for two hours each morning and another two to three hours in the evenings, which left enough time to prepare meals and keep the house running. I was slow at first, but it didn't take long to bring myself back up to speed, and the typewriter's familiar cadence was calming. It muffled the sounds of the house—the airy rasp of Michael's oxygen mask, the chatter of the television, the drone of the dryer. Typing didn't eliminate my dread of the sentencing date, but it was a way to focus the nervous energy buzzing behind my temples, like a hive of angry bees.

---

CASA scheduled a meeting for December 22, so those of us who had given our victim impact statements could debrief. I wasn't planning to go. I had just started typing Monty's manuscript, and for the first time in years, I was looking forward to Christmas. I wanted to focus on the preparations for Christmas dinner at

Neil's House with Chris, Mila, Michael, and Monty. I wanted to wrap gifts and bake Nanaimo bars and pumpkin pie. I was even looking forward to spending the twenty-fourth with Rachel and my parents. I hadn't seen them since the day in court, but my mother had phoned. She didn't say a word about my statement, but she asked if there was anything special I would like for Christmas. I wanted to think that was her way of reaching out. It might be strained, but I knew we would celebrate Christmas like any other year. So rehashing that day in court, going over the same sad stories with the same sad people at CASA, could wait.

Then Eva, one of the leaders at CASA, called with a reminder about the meeting. I made thin excuses. "Come anyway," she said. "We need you."

I wanted to be done with the support group. I was tired of talking about Father and the Church and court cases and abuse and lies and all our messed up feelings about it all. But Eva's *we need you* echoed. I needed them as much as they needed me. Maybe more.

In a nod to the holidays, cookies and eggnog replaced the urn of weak coffee, and we mingled for a while before taking our seats in the circle. Maybe it was the aftershock of reading our victim impact statements, or anticipation of the holidays, or a combination of the two, but the emotional tone as we waited to get started was unlike that of past meetings, somewhere now between trepidation and celebration. We tried too hard to make small talk. Then we wept and sighed. Some people ranted at top volume and others sank quietly into woolly turtlenecks. I kept my hands in my pockets and made an effort to smile, nod, or frown at the right times. I wanted the official part of the meeting to begin, needed the security of the metal folding chair under me.

I had been so distracted in court that I hadn't heard the other statements, but I could tell others had taken in every word that day, including mine. I was one of the younger CASA members, and as I listened, I realized my story was different from the others. Father had preyed on others at church and at school. But in my case, he had also insinuated himself into our family and was in our house so often that he had access to me everywhere—at church, at school, and at home.

*Your statement was so powerful.... So honest.... So brave,* they said.

*Thank you,* I said. *You too.* All I could think was, *Thank God it's over. Behind us.*

When we finally took our seats, Eva said, "I'd like us to consider inviting Alex Bain to our January meeting. She's a lawyer who has dealt with these cases in other dioceses. She can explain what a civil suit will entail. I think this is the natural next step moving forward."

The air rushed from my lungs. What did she mean by "moving forward?" Moving forward meant Father would be sentenced and go to jail. Moving forward meant no more trials and victim impact statements and reporters and waiting and nightmares and insomnia. It meant not thinking about doing all the dysfunctional things I did when I was younger, like cutting my inner thigh with an X-Acto blade, just a tiny bit, to see if it still felt the same, to see if that trickle of blood still brought a surge of release. Moving forward meant doing normal things, simple things, like cooking and shopping and taking care of Michael and typing for Monty and doing those things because I wanted to do them, I was happy doing them, and not because I was trying to distract myself from the terrifying images that came when I was alone with my fucked-up thoughts. And it meant when I was with people, people other than Chris and Mila and Rachel, they wouldn't look at me like I was messed up or broken, like I was a pathetic victim, because that was in the past, the distant past, because I had moved forward, moved on, and now I got to have a normal life, a life where I would open the newspaper and read my horoscope, and it would say, *Things are looking up,* and they actually would be.

I looked around. Everyone else was looking at Eva, nodding in agreement. A woman with curly red hair said, "I think it's good to find out more about a civil suit. But what about the Church? It's one thing for one pedophile priest to go to jail, but the way I see it, it's not all on him. The Church, the Bishop, other priests—they covered for that creep all those years. We need to do something about that."

I felt anxious and angry and frustrated. *Moving forward* really meant going back, it seemed. I tried to swallow the laughter rising in my throat, but it burbled up and out. Everyone stared.

---

Mila and Monty firmed up their holiday plans. "Just something low-key," they said. "The evening of the twenty-fifth. We'll have a fondue, a few bottles of wine. Rachel can come, and Sara—they're friends, right?—and maybe some of the other volunteers, if they're free." I was happy Neil's House felt like home to them too.

When Rachel and I were young, Christmas glittered and shone. The house felt extra cozy, and we wore flannel pajamas for days. Sweet scents of cinnamon and nutmeg, cocoa and caramel, ginger and molasses wafted from the kitchen, perfuming every room. We decorated the tree with red and green glass ornaments and strings of twinkle lights, then draped tinsel on each branch, one glittering strand at a time. Dad circled our favorite Christmas specials in the *TV Guide*, and we sat on the floor in front of the television with bowls of popcorn in our laps watching *Frosty the Snowman*, *Rudolph the Red-Nosed Reindeer*, and *How the Grinch Stole Christmas!* Gran, my mother's mother, came from North Bay on the train bearing old-fashioned gifts: crocheted finger puppet animals, paper dolls, and tins of watercolor paints. Whatever other presents appeared under the tree, these were our favorites.

Starting the year I turned eight, Gran stayed home with Rachel on Christmas Eve, and I went to Midnight Mass with my parents. The service began in darkness. Each person held a candle, and starting at the back of the church, a flame was passed from wick to wick to wick, until flickering golden light filled the nave. I remember standing between my parents that first year and holding my candle steady. It was long past my bedtime, and in my dreamy state, the warm, wavering glow softened the cathedral's sharp edges. When tiny drops of hot wax slid down the taper and onto my knuckles, I didn't flinch. Instead, I bit my bottom lip and watched the beads of wax harden as they cooled. Not only was I a *Good Girl*, but going to Midnight Mass meant I was also *Grown Up*, and I knew that meant you didn't whine or complain. I knew it meant I must keep still and quiet, even if it was difficult, even if I bit my lip a little too hard and saliva and blood trickled down my throat and pooled in the pit of my stomach. Even then. Because when I looked around, I could lose myself in the shimmering candlelight and heady incense and fold myself into the reverent fold.

The magic of the holiday had worn off. Still, Christmas was not just another day. Mila and Monty were excited about their gathering on the twenty-fifth, and on the twenty-fourth, Rachel and I went to Midnight Mass with our parents. We sat in the overheated cathedral, wedged in, shoulder-to-shoulder. Since giving my victim impact statement, the swarm and buzz of crowds overwhelmed me. There was no way to anticipate or avoid the sting of judgment. I sank down into the fur-trimmed hood of my parka. Rachel sat beside me, her thigh tight against mine, and when I looked at her, she rolled her eyes, then winked conspiratorially. I held Rachel's gaze and forced a weak smile. I knew she didn't want to be there either, that she would rather be with her friends. And Sara. Though she hadn't come out in so many words, I knew she and Sara were a couple. I was happy for her, for them both, but I was also jealous. I couldn't see it at the time, but

I envied their relationship. I wasn't anywhere near ready to have a partner, but I sometimes looked at Chris and Mila and wondered what that kind of love and trust would feel like. Mostly, I missed Rachel, and resented the time she spent with Sara. In moments of self-pity, I hoped they would break up so I would have Rachel all to myself again.

I looked up at a stained-glass window depicting the image of Saint Rita, a pretty nun with a glowing stigmata in the center of her forehead. I dug my thumbnail into the palm of my hand, a self-imposed penance for my uncharitable thoughts.

When we stood for the gospel reading, my knees buckled and I sat back down. Rachel sat too and unzipped my coat a little. "Are you okay?" she whispered. Our mother glared at us and motioned for us to stand.

"I've got to go," I said. When the congregation sat for the homily, I stumbled past my parents and into the aisle and hurried out the rear entrance of the cathedral.

Rachel caught up with me. "What happened in there?" she asked.

"I don't know. I'm just done," I said. "I just can't...."

"It's okay," she said, wrapping her arms around me. "You don't have to."

We stood on the sidewalk in front of the cathedral for a long time. The night was cold and still, and snow fell in large, soft flakes, like dandelion fluff. Finally I said, "Let's go home."

"Home?" she said. "You mean our house or Neil's House?"

"Our house. It's Christmas Eve. I can do that much." I knew things would be fine when my parents came home. They would ask if I was feeling better, and my mother would tell me I should have taken off my coat, that I had overheated. We would go on with the evening. We would eat and exchange gifts and make small talk like nothing had happened, like it was any other Christmas, like we were any other family.

"Come on," I said. "We'll walk."

As Rachel and I walked away from the cathedral, I glanced back over my shoulder. The snow had covered our footprints completely, as though we had never been there.

On the tenth of January, the day of the sentencing, I stayed home. I typed until my shoulders sagged and ached, then I sat on the sofa with the manuscript and proofread twelve chapters. By the time I finished, it was late afternoon. I was just about to correct a few typos when Eva phoned.

"Three years," she said. "The judge gave him three years. He said the sentence was mitigated by Father's advanced age and poor health. It's so wrong. It's just so wrong."

I thanked her for calling and hung up.

I did the math. Three years. Twenty-seven days for each of us. It took a few minutes to sink in. It wasn't possible to add up all the times Father had preyed on all of us, in his office at the rectory, in the dark corners of the school auditorium, in cars and confessionals and little girls' bedrooms. But if each incident were tallied, the sentence would be negligible, a trifling penance for his decades of heinous crimes. I didn't know what I had expected, but it was more than this. We were worth more than this.

I ran upstairs, laid face down on my bed, and wept silent tears. I could have screamed. But if I did, I might never stop.

Stories about Father ran in every newspaper. I went to the corner store, bought them all, and spread them across my bedroom floor. *The most shocking priest-pedophile case to date*, the papers said. *Record number of victims. Sentence sparks criticism from victims' rights groups.* I closed my eyes. I opened them and read some more. I could only read for so long before anger twisted the words into an indecipherable black cloud.

Worse than the articles were the photographs of Father that accompanied them. Some papers ran one picture, some two, most in black and white, a few in color.

One was a portrait taken when Father was a young priest, probably at the time of his ordination or the posting to his first parish. In this photo, Father looked directly into the camera. He was strikingly handsome, clean-shaven, and rosy-cheeked. His eyes sparkled and his teeth gleamed. His hair was neatly combed and shiny with pomade, his sideburns perfectly squared. But for the Roman collar, he could be the running back on a college football team or the heroic doctor in a 1960s medical drama. He was the epitome of clean-cut goodness and virtue, a model cleric. Though it was decades old, I recognized the photo because the papers had used it for years, alongside stories about church fundraisers or Father's reappointments within the diocese. The same one hung in parish halls and school foyers. His parents would have displayed this picture in a gold frame set front and center on the mantel, winning the envy of his mother's friends whose sons were mere accountants and lawyers. His grandmother would have placed it on her nightstand beside her missal and rosary and dusted it daily with soft, gray flannel.

The second photo was similar in style to the first: a traditional portrait in black and white. It was probably taken for a parish directory and used in the weekly bulletin. Though Father was older in this photo—perhaps in his late forties—he was still very good-looking. His hairline had receded only slightly, and he had not gone gray. His skin was taut but for fine lines at the corners of his eyes, and his smile was just the same. In this photo, Father gazed past the camera, above and beyond. "Look here," the photographer would have said, raising his hand in the air, so that anyone who looked at the photo would understand Father's authority. His pious confidence left no doubt of his elevated status in this world and beyond.

The third was not a portrait; it appeared to have been taken outside the courthouse. Father clutched a prayer book to his chest. Everything about him was thin: his hair, his lips, his neck. His Roman collar and dark jacket looked as though they were borrowed from a much larger man. His eyes were pale and round. He looked at the camera, but it was difficult to read his expression. He had been caught off guard by the photographer. After more than forty years as a priest, he was accustomed to being the center of attention, but the assault of reporters was unfamiliar. He was taken aback, off-balance.

I suppose those photos were meant to draw the reader in, to put a face to the crimes. But they made me seethe with hatred. I'd been angry before, but I'd never felt it so completely, in every nerve ending, every pore. My skin was hot with rage, and I pulled on my jacket and walked around the block. The winter air tempered my fury. I wondered how others saw the photos. Were they angry too? Or did they feel reverence? Or pity? Did they see a holy man? A victim? A monster? A twisted hybrid of saint and sinner?

---

CASA learned that the Bishop was coming to say mass at the cathedral, to speak about Father's case and the church's plan for healing. We organized a silent vigil. We would stand on the sidewalk in front of the cathedral, survivors and supporters together, holding signs:

SUPPORT VICTIMS

RELEASE THE NAMES OF
ALL PEDOPHILE PRIESTS

WE WILL NOT BE SILENCED!

SHAME ON THE RC CHURCH!

The night before, I told Chris I wasn't going. "I gave my statement. That's enough." Even as I said it, I knew it wasn't true. Once the initial anger at Father's sentencing subsided, I felt jaded and tired.

"It's more than enough." Chris paused. "But if you want me to go with you, I can."

"That's the thing—no one should have to go. Not me, not you, not anyone. It's just one more thing on top of the thousands of other shitty things we've had to do, all because of that creep. When's it going to end?" I heard my voice, shrill and angry, and took a deep breath. "I'm a broken record, I know. You must get tired of hearing about it."

"You know," Chris said, "I've been thinking. Those of us who think we are on the outside are not really so far removed. The abuse that man inflicted on children in this city impacted us all. Not in the same ways, but we've all been affected, and we need to stand together and see this through. That's the only way real change happens. I'm no expert, but I see the way attitudes have been changing, just a little, toward my patients. And that's only happened because people came together, lobbied the government, took to the streets, made some noise. Absolutely no judgment if you don't go tomorrow. Your needs come first, and you have to do what's best for you. But I'm going to go anyway. I want to. Don't decide tonight. Sleep on it."

I knew before I fell asleep that I would go. I still didn't *want* to go, and it would still be awful, but Chris's support made me feel just a little stronger.

The next morning, we stood together, staring straight ahead, our shoulders squared. A few CASA members were no-shows, and I understood because I had come so close to staying home too. We wore black, the color of loss and anger. *We are here. You cannot ignore us.* When people arrived for mass, they were not sure where to look. Some were noticeably uncomfortable and scuttled past like sand crabs. Others, pious and indignant, held their heads high and breezed by as though we were not there, as though we were the ghosts of ghosts. I felt exposed and invisible at the same time.

The Bishop had been ushered in through the back entrance. The organ pumped "Faith of Our Fathers" clear to the sidewalk. *Jesus Christ,* someone behind me muttered. *That's just perfect.*

---

Alex Bain came to a CASA meeting and advised us to meet with the Bishop. In her legal opinion, it was in the best interest of the diocese to settle out of court and avoid the publicity of a civil suit, especially after Father's guilty plea. "It might be a good resolution for you as well," she added. "Though that's a decision you have to make, as individuals and as a collective."

We decided to meet with the Bishop. For most of us, this was not our first time. We had been to his office years ago, alone or with our parents, only a few of us with lawyers. Like so many people—some we knew and even more we didn't—we had sat across from the Bishop and disclosed our long-held secrets. For years, we had been shamed into silence, but then we told the truth. Some of us cried and pleaded. Some of us cursed and pounded the table. A few of us stormed out. Our suffering was appraised. *Compensation for your time,* we were told, *for any discomfort this misunderstanding may have caused.* We signed away our stories and took our checks to the bank. We thought the worst was behind us. We believed we'd had our day.

But this time, we went together. We crowded into a large rental van, which made the day feel like an ill-conceived field trip. When we arrived at the chancellery office, the Bishop's secretary ushered us into a softly lit boardroom where we sat around a gleaming mahogany table. We waited. The only sound came from the air vent, its gentle whirr drawing attention to the chill in the room. We glanced at one another, but no one spoke.

Finally, a priest arrived, flanked by sober men in three-piece suits. The priest was familiar: He was the spokesman for the diocese, and he appeared regularly on the television news. "Good morning. Sorry to keep you waiting," he said, smiling as though he knew nothing of sorrow or waiting. He took his seat at the head of the table. "His Eminence has been called away. He sends his regrets but has asked that we use this time to have a preliminary discussion."

Some of the women at the table huffed and scoffed at the news of the Bishop's absence. I squirmed uncomfortably in my seat. I shared their frustration, but I was also relieved not to have to see him, not to have to swallow a toxic mix of fear and anger yet again.

"Let us begin with a prayer." The priest extended his palms and cleared his throat. "Heavenly Father, we gather here today in a spirit of healing...."

Everyone bowed their heads and closed their eyes, some out of respect, some out of habit. As the priest droned on, I stopped listening. I opened one eye to look at him. His eyes were closed, his spotless white hands raised in supplication. He wore a Roman collar, but his shirt was pale yellow, not black. I suspected this was intentional, an attempt to set himself apart from his peers with their black shirts and soutanes. He was young—forty or so. Young for a priest. I noticed a tiny scar on his earlobe, a healed-over piercing. I wondered if there were others, nipple piercings maybe, which made me want to laugh. When I suppressed the laughter, it sounded like a sob, and the lawyers fidgeted uncomfortably. The priest did not notice, absorbed in prayer or the sound of his own voice.

I took a deep breath and tried to focus on the present, how it was almost time for victims everywhere to speak, to start telling the world all the secrets we had been paid to keep quiet. We knew about the Christian Brothers at Mount Cashel, and we knew there were survivors' groups forming around the world. We had all been told our nondisclosure agreements were ironclad, irrevocable. But the Church had not upheld Her end of the deal. From Father-in-the-Yellow-Shirt all the way up to the Pope himself, so many Fathers had covered up for so many Fathers.

Soon, everyone would know.

---

One afternoon, a courier delivered a large, flat package wrapped in brown paper. It was addressed to Neil's House; there was no return address. I set it on the kitchen table, reluctant to open it. I gave it a wide berth, as though it were a scorpion or a bomb. When Chris arrived home, we stared at it together.

"Well, let's do this," she said finally and sliced the paper with a paring knife. Inside the unmarked box, wrapped in layers of bubble wrap, was a framed certificate set in rich matting, much like a university diploma in size and style. Chris lifted the heavy frame from the box.

IN RECOGNITION OF THEIR OUTSTANDING
CONTRIBUTIONS TO THE LOCAL COMMUNITY
THE MAYOR AND CITY COUNCIL
PROUDLY NAME
THE FOUNDERS AND VOLUNTEERS OF NEIL'S HOUSE
CITIZENS OF THE YEAR

Chris slowly shook her head. "How?"

"Who?" I asked.

I searched the box and found a plain white envelope. Inside was a check for five thousand dollars made out to me and Chris.

Chris laid the frame on the table. "This doesn't make any sense. Who even knows we're here?"

I told Chris about my conversation with Kurt Hennessy. "I meant to tell you about this sooner, but Monty had just moved in and then it slipped my mind, you know? But if you think about it, we have about fifteen volunteers now, and we've had twenty-one residents over the past three years, and some of their friends and family know about us."

"Don't get me wrong—the recognition is nice. And so is the money," Chris said. "But like I've said before, we have to be prepared for what might happen next. Public health will be breathing down our necks in no time." Chris sat down and ran her hands through her hair. "Mostly, I worry about what publicity will do to the safety of our residents. There's still a lot of misinformation out there. And people can be cruel."

I wanted to say maybe things had changed enough that we could be less guarded, that people knew more, that they weren't as ignorant or scared. But I didn't know that for sure. If I had learned one thing from going to court, it was that some people were motivated by compassion and others by fear or hatred.

---

And then Michael died. He had been with us for almost a year, and in his last few months, he had faded to gray, like an old photograph. He died in his sleep, alone. A heavy sadness blanketed the house. Chris and I were as adrift as Bustopher, who spent hours roaming from room to room. I held him close and buried my face in his fur.

Most of the men who stayed at Neil's House did not have funerals. The coroner's office collected their bodies, and they were cremated without ceremony and buried in unmarked graves. Even in death, they were shrouded in shame and secrecy. Each time a resident died, Chris lit a small red votive candle. These lined the mantel, a simple shrine to their too short lives.

When Chris called Michael's parents, they arranged for a funeral home in a neighboring city to pick up his body. They planned a funeral at an Anglican church, followed by a gathering for family and friends. "Please come," they said. "You meant so much to Michael, and to us." I'd only met his parents once, briefly, when Michael moved in. I knew he had a sister in Winnipeg. Michael kept a picture of her family, including her two young children, on his dresser. He seldom spoke of them, and when he did, he said little. He wasn't our only resident who had been reluctant to speak of his family. In fact, most were selective in the stories they shared. Even Neil had been reticent to talk about his illness or his past, as though bound by a code of silence. Neil's House had afforded Michael and the other residents the dignity of a supportive community, a place they were loved and cared for, but that didn't mean they felt safe acknowledging the outside world where they risked the hurt of rejection.

As we drove to the funeral, Chris said, "I'm surprised they're having a service. I know Michael talked to his family on the phone sometimes, but they didn't care enough to come around. They weren't there for him when he was alive."

I didn't reply. It was hard to accept Chris's assessment. Part of me wanted to defend Michael's parents, to make excuses for their absence. I'd done that often enough with my own parents, telling myself they just weren't ready, they needed more time to come to terms with the past, the court case, my brokenness. I hated to consider it, but maybe, like Michael's parents, even if my parents cared, they didn't care enough.

By the end of the afternoon, I realized we couldn't have been more wrong about Michael's family. The funeral was impersonal, led by a priest who clearly did not know Michael. But at the luncheon that followed, everyone spoke lovingly about Michael. They described him as generous and thoughtful, adventurous and funny, humble and kind. Their sorrow ran deep and tears flowed freely. Michael's father offered a short eulogy. "We couldn't be with Michael at the end," he said, "but we know we were in his heart, as he was in ours. He told his mother and me he didn't want to be a burden. He didn't want us to see him sick. We tried to respect Michael's wishes, tried to understand. But we would have done anything for him. He was our only son, our beautiful boy. We were so proud of him. He was a straight-A student, a gifted artist. And he had the biggest heart, from the time he was a kid. He always looked out for his little sister and he had so many friends. He took in every stray cat in the neighborhood. He grew up to be a good man, a loving partner to Dave. He took such good care of Dave when he got sick. We wish we could have done the same for Michael...."

Chris and I had assumed Michael's family had distanced themselves from Michael, but it turned out the opposite was true. That Michael spoke of them infrequently, that they didn't visit, was not a reflection of indifference or prejudice but about Michael trying to protect them—and himself.

I knew we hadn't created the gulf between Michael and his family. But we hadn't bridged it either, hadn't provided passage from one shore to the other. For more than two years, we had tried so hard to protect Neil's House and its residents, to ensure their privacy and safety, but maybe it was time to try a new way, to test the waters and navigate the currents of change.

Monty moved back to his home. As Chris had predicted, his new drug cocktail was effective and he was noticeably stronger. He probably could have gone home sooner, but it was convenient to be in the same house as I transcribed his draft, and I think he enjoyed the company. When Monty moved out, two new residents moved in—Marcel, for a short-term stay while his doctors figured out a medication regimen, and Cary, who was very ill and near the end.

With Monty no longer in residence, Chris and I began to talk about how Neil's House might go public. We held a meeting with the volunteers. We invited Kurt and a few other members of the local Gay and Lesbian Association to tour the house. The consensus was that, with our committed volunteers and a community group willing to fundraise, it was time to move forward with a plan to turn Neil's House into an accredited hospice.

Over and over again, Chris said, "I can't believe how far we've come."

I couldn't believe it either. I remembered when Neil was ill, and Chris came to the house for the first time. I had known she was coming and met her at the kitchen door. She smiled and said, "You must be Neil's assistant." And before I could answer, she began pulling files from her bag and explaining Neil's care plan, medications, and what to expect in the weeks and months ahead. I had been overwhelmed, but relieved too. I needed Chris; she had experience and confidence at a time when I had none. My worry proved unnecessary, but at the time, I feared that opening the door to her help might somehow expose Neil to judgment or harm. I was used to closed doors, comfortable with them. But they hadn't always protected me. In fact, many times, they had done just the opposite. And now I felt a similar unease; the difference was, I wouldn't face the next challenges alone.

A month after we met with The-Priest-in-the-Yellow-Shirt, Alex Bain presented the Bishop's offer. To avoid a lawsuit, the diocese was prepared to release Father's victims from their nondisclosure agreements and pay a group compensation of fifteen million dollars. Divided among the nearly four dozen victims, and taking into consideration our legal costs and future victim claims, we would each receive about $200,000. Some were ready to accept the settlement and put the past behind them, but others were not. We met with Alex long into the night. In the end, many of us took the settlement and a small group moved forward with a civil suit. I took the money, but I didn't look with judgment on the women who did not. The settlement didn't fix or heal or soothe. But in the past, when I'd wanted to move on, I was really just running away. Now, I'd told my story, and I had something to move on to. And if the money could help fund a new Neil's House, maybe that was the best I could do.

I talked to my former colleagues at Holmes Realty and put Neil's house on the market. It was an easy decision. I was attached to the memories but not the house.

In no time, people came together, committees met, a Board of Directors formed and elected Chris as its Chair. She had returned from the International AIDS Conference in Montreal with inspiration and ideas to spare, and her enthusiasm fueled and energized us. At Chris's urging, I volunteered to serve on the Building Subcommittee. Though I lacked the credentials of the accountant, architect, interior designer, and other professionals on the committee, I had one important qualification: I knew Neil better than anyone, and everyone agreed that finding ways to incorporate Neil's love of literature and art into the building would be a way to honor him.

A well-equipped hospice required considerably more space. The Building Subcommittee viewed several sites. The most promising was an old eight-room elementary school. Located in the center of the city, it had been abandoned as middle-class families migrated to new upscale housing developments in the suburbs. I toured the school with Chris and several others. In one of the classrooms, I ran my finger along a dust-covered chalkboard ledge. I looked into the cloakroom, empty but for a pair of tattered sneakers. A photograph of the Pope hung above the blackboard. He looked down on the room with twinkling blue eyes and a grandfatherly smile, oblivious to anything and everything that had happened on his watch. I turned my back and waited in the hall for the others. I leaned against the cool brick and closed my eyes. Though vacant for years, it still smelled like a school—a musty pong of glue, sour milk, disinfectant, and wet boots. In kindergarten, this had been a hopeful scent; by first grade, it was infused with fear and trepidation. Like the odor itself, that fear was indelible; there was no point in trying to mask or defeat it. It would always be there.

After the tour of the site, we sat around the dining room table at Neil's House. The architect who sat on the board described how each classroom could be divided into two bedrooms and the existing plumbing easily extended to accommodate a private bath for each. If we renovated for a ten-bed hospice, we would still have plenty of space for offices, a nurses' station, a kitchen, and a large communal lounge.

"It's perfect," Chris said. The range of her vision exceeded mine, but I was happy to take her lead. She saw Neil's House not only as a hospice, but also as a community center that would offer outreach and education programs. A place for life as well as death.

When the location of the new Neil's House became known, we met with resistance, much of it predictable. Neighbors were concerned that a hospice would increase traffic in the area, but their not-in-my-backyard arguments were easily countered. More alarming were the hate-filled letters to the editor, condemning AIDS as *God's punishment for homosexuality.* We knew such homophobic attitudes existed, but after years of operating Neil's House covertly, it was distressing to be the target of such poisonous rhetoric.

During the renovation, the site was vandalized. Someone spray-painted FAGGOTS across the front doors. The Board called an emergency meeting, and some members arrived with pails and wire brushes. "Let's leave it for a few days," Chris said. "Give people time to think about how hateful it is. Maybe it will change minds." The next week, an art teacher from the nearby high school showed up with a few students and offered to paint the doors. When they were done, a vibrant rainbow stretched across the double doors and onto the dingy, beige brick.

At each stage of the project, new volunteers appeared. They arrived with time, energy, skills, and financial generosity toward people they didn't know and likely would never meet. Architects, plumbers, electricians, carpenters, tilers, drywallers, painters, and interior designers transformed the building. Week after week, more people arrived. They scoured and scrubbed, mopped and swept. Artists painted the halls with vivid murals of gardens and sunny skies. A quilting league stitched ten colorful quilts. The Gay Men's Chorus organized a gala. Service clubs ran lotteries and silent auctions. A marching band held a band-a-thon, and a dance troupe a dance-a-thon. A junior high school held a bake sale, and a seven-year-old girl emptied her penny jar. A woman whose grandson had died from AIDS sold her 1964 Mustang and donated the proceeds.

So much had changed. The activity of planning, renovating, and organizing seemed to whirl around me. I marvelled at the improbable evolution of Neil's House—the building as well as the people. During the last months of Neil's life, he and I were alone except for Chris and a few other home care nurses. I'd come to understand that Neil had planned his death that way, that he had chosen to disconnect and isolate, because he was afraid or ashamed. I wondered what choices he might have made if he had been granted a few more years. *Hindsight is a gift*, I thought. I still tried to block out certain memories, still squeezed my eyes tight, and buried my head under the pillow most nights trying to keep the past at bay. I had a long way to go, but at least I had time, support, and new purpose with the work of Neil's House.

I flipped the kitchen calendar from May to June and scanned the month ahead. Soon, I would turn twenty-five. I sighed. For nineteen of those years, the worst days of my life had eclipsed all others. I spent so much time worrying about when the next worst thing would happen, wondering when it would stop, when it would go away. I monitored my thoughts and movements, anticipated threats, weighed risks, and second-guessed every decision. I learned to spot danger in the most innocuous situations. I smiled through fear and self-loathing. I rationed my words and rarely took a full breath. I was awkward and backward in every way, or so it seemed to me. I said *yes* when I meant *no* and *no* when I meant *yes*. Well beyond the years when I was technically a girl, teachers and parents offered rote praise—*Good Girl, Good Girl*—though deep down, I knew I could never be *good* nor *girl* enough, no matter how hard I tried. In nineteen years, three quarters of my life, all the usual rites of passage—sacraments, graduations, the severing of apron strings—had left me unchanged. I was almost two decades older, but my six-year-old self still looked over my shoulder, fully expecting the past to catch up. If I kept looking back, would I ever choose a career, fall in love, make a life for myself? I loved my work with Neil's House, but it wouldn't need me forever.

I was still staring at the calendar when Mila came into the kitchen. She stood behind me and rested her chin on my shoulder. "What are we looking at?"

"June," I said.

"My birthday's the twelfth," said Mila.

"Mine's the fourteenth."

"We should plan a little party. Or a big party! At a club! I could get a band!" Mila's enthusiasm expanded to fill the room.

"Honestly, I'm not really into celebrating my birthday. My parents will have me over for cake. That's enough."

"Not this year," Mila said. "This year we need to celebrate our birthdays—and the big move. We'll invite a few friends, all the volunteers, Monty.... I'll make a list. Should we have it here or at a club? Or maybe a restaurant?"

"Really, Mila. Let's not. Birthdays are depressing."

"What's that now?" Mila asked.

"I'll be twenty-five. My birthday will just remind me of all the things I haven't done. I didn't go to college. I haven't travelled. I've never even been on a date."

"First of all, twenty-five is young. You have lots of time for all those things. And besides, you've done more than a lot of people do in a lifetime! You founded a hospice, for Pete's sake. And you managed it too. Think of all the good you've done, all the lives you've touched. And the new Neil's House? That was possible because of you. You're remarkable, my friend."

It was difficult to hear those words, hard to accept Mila's assessment and praise. Of course I was happy about all that had happened in the past six months, and watching Neil's House take shape was rewarding. But there were times at the end of the day when I felt more than just tired. I carried a weight with me, a heavy cross, and I wasn't sure how or where to set it down. I wasn't naïve; I knew the abuse I endured would always be with me, and I knew the relationship with my parents would never be the same. Still, something had to change. I just wasn't sure how to begin.

# [PART 4]

*In the Beginning was the Word, and the Word was with God, and the Word was God.* What could be more reliable? But in time, words echo and fade away, carried off on the wind, blown to the four corners. Words can be as ineffectual as they are powerful, as flimsy as they are concrete.

From first days, parents coo and whisper into tiny ears. You're never too young to learn. *Say Mama. Say Dada. Say juice* and *please* and *up. Say thank you. Say you're sorry. Say your prayers.* Saying the right words at the right time in the right place is praiseworthy. From a person's first word to their last, speech is as fundamental as breath. *Loquor ergo sum.* You are the sum of your syllables.

Consider the great orators of the modern era: Sojourner Truth, Mohandas Gandhi, Martin Luther King Jr., Gloria Steinem. They are the voices of their generations, and their words will endure on paper and in digital code. Back in the thirteenth century, Saint Anthony, a Franciscan priest, preached so eloquently that schools of fishes amassed along the shore to listen to his sermons.

Today, his tongue, jawbone, and vocal cords are enshrined in a basilica in Padua, Italy, inspiration to speechless pilgrims. Saint Anthony's miraculous ability is a rarity, unrivalled by modern wordsmiths.

Words are sustenance, succor, salve. Committed to the page, the language of love would fill a million notebooks. *How do I love thee? Let me count the ways....* But take caution: The same words used to woo might be used to deceive. Like con artists and unfaithful spouses, words are unreliable. They wound as often as they soothe. Speech packs a potent punch.

Words can fail us at our most desperate moments, go into exile like political dissidents. Spells and incantations lose their power; prayers and mantras are futile. Witnesses *swear to tell the truth and nothing but the truth.* But this is easier said than done. It's not the swearing or the truth that poses the challenge. It's the telling.

Nondisclosure begins as a safety net; eventually it becomes a snarled, sticky web. AIDS activists pasted pink triangle posters on lampposts. *Silence = Death*, an equation proven true more than forty million times.

Too often, silence seeps under the skin, coursing through every capillary, seeping into our viscera and marrow, altering affect and psyche. In a word-weary world, psychoanalysis, the talking cure, might lead to catharsis—but only for those who can locate banished words and speak them in somber, cautious tones. Still, sometimes, there are no words.

# [1991]

Therapy was not what I expected. When people at CASA talked about the benefits of counselling, I pictured them sitting on a leather couch while a bespectacled, bearded man jotted in a notebook. But it turned out to be nothing like that. It was just me and Dr. LaRue, talking. Every Thursday at ten, month after month, in comfortable armchairs in her sunny office, while her fluffy mop of a dog slept on the floor between us.

At first, we made small talk and I thought, *I can do this.* In time, the intensity of our hours increased, and I started to feel like Rico, one of the residents at Neil's House. Rico came to us after he collapsed in his kitchen and knocked a boiling pot from the stove. His torso and thighs were covered in second- and third-degree burns, and because of his HIV status, his chances of infection were especially high. He stayed in the hospital for a few days, then was discharged to Chris's care. Each day, we donned surgical masks and gloves, and I assisted while Chris debrided his burns. Rico lay perfectly still, his eyes closed, as she irrigated the burns and used fine tweezers to remove the charred, dead tissue. I held a small stainless-steel basin and watched in silence as it filled with pinkish-gray flakes. Just witnessing the process was painful, and the scar on my hand tingled in empathy. Rico and Chris were exhausted by the end. But in a few weeks, Rico's burns began to heal, and tight, shiny scars covered the area.

Therapy was a psychological debridement. Session after session, Dr. LaRue nudged and probed to expose a wound, then carefully excised a sliver of raw memory to examine under a microscope. *What happened?* she'd ask. And I would tell her a story, often about Father but sometimes about school or church or my parents or Rachel or Neil. *Look closer*, she'd say, pointing out some minor detail. *What do you see now?* I would squint and adjust my focus. Words caught and tangled in my throat. When I couldn't speak, she filled in the answers: *That's Coercion.... That's Anger.... That's Self-preservation.... That's Grief.... That's Love.*

My injuries had only just started to heal. In recent years, they had scabbed over several times, only to have the scabs knocked off and the wounds exposed. The long, steady process of therapy allowed tender scars to form, on the surface and deep within, where they were evident to some but not to others. Those scars would always be there, visceral reminders of tragedy and loss and healing.

---

When Chris, Mila, and I moved from Neil's house, I rented an apartment across town near the lake. I took Bustopher with me. When anyone asked about my new place, I offered a neutral response: *It's getting there* or *It's comfortable.* I was embarrassed to show my naïve delight in something so ordinary. Each time I walked through the door, I felt a tiny shiver of pleasure, even after months of living there. I never tired of running my hands over the dining table, or admiring the colorful pillows on my new bed, or rearranging photos and books. Monty had mentioned me in the acknowledgments of his new novel, and I placed it front and center on my bookshelf. I read for hours in the bath. I ate when I was hungry and napped when I was tired. I felt like I was on vacation. Bustopher seemed content too: He spent his days grooming and playing in the sunny living room, then curled up with me on the couch at night.

Rachel and Sara lived just down the street in student housing. Rachel was in her first year in the nursing program at the college, and Sara worked in Dietary Services at the hospital. They beamed like newlyweds, and as I spent more time with them, Sara became as much a sister to me as Rachel. Chris and Mila bought a house just outside the city. Mila stopped touring with the band and opened a small recording studio. They invited me for dinner often, and most times, I accepted. I wondered if they invited me because they thought I was lonely, but I wasn't. There were times I missed the communal living of the first Neil's House, but I enjoyed having my own space. It was time I lived on my own.

The feeling that I was living someone else's happy life crested most days around four or five in the afternoon. I felt a change in the air as the weight of evening descended. I watched television late into the night and fell asleep on the couch. Maybe it was the glow of the television or the moonlight, but I slept lightly in the living room, and this seemed to keep the terrifying nightmares at bay. To avoid waking up with a gasp, soaked in perspiration and shivering, I slept on the couch every night, then hid my sheets and blanket away in the linen cupboard each morning. The pretty pillows on my bed rested undisturbed.

Still, sometimes I slid too deeply into sleep and nightmares found me. In sleep, my memories of family dinners, holiday parties, and church socials contorted into vivid, violent dreams.

I shared some of them with Dr. LaRue but kept others to myself.

*I am a child but in my adult body, watching from the edge of the room. Music, laughter, the clinking of glasses, then a sudden, overwhelming fear that pierces my eardrums like a smoke alarm. I wait, knowing something is about to happen, but unsure what. Father's laughter rises above the din, and I freeze. I can't see him but know he is there. I turn to leave but can't find the door. I spin full-circle, and everyone else has disappeared. Father is blocking the exit. He places his hands on my shoulders, turns me away from him, and grinds against me. I see the door now. It is ajar, and I will someone to come. I hear footsteps. Father lets go of me as someone closes the door with a click. I turn around, and the room falls silent. I grab the closest object—a pen, a fork, a broken plate—and lunge at Father. He stands, unmoving, arms outstretched as I flail and slash and stab.*

Two mornings a week I volunteered at Neil's House, helping Chris in the office. I typed and filed, and when time permitted, I worked on my pet project: collecting and organizing a small library of books, magazines, and movies for the residents. I was affixing labels to some new videotapes when Terry, one of the nurses, asked if I would stop in on a resident. "John in Room 4 is asking for some books, and I'm not really sure what they are. A *breviary* and a *missal?*"

"They're Catholic prayer books. I'll see what I can find." We didn't keep many religious books in our little library, but I knew my mother would either have them or be able to get them from the church.

The door to Room 4 was open, so I knocked lightly on the frame. "Hello," I said softly. "John? The nurse mentioned you're looking for some books."

"Oh, yes, come in, come in. Terry said you would be by." John sat upright on the bed, propped by several pillows. He was pale, and his cheeks were hollow, but his silver hair was combed neatly, and his eyes were bright. He set aside a book of crossword puzzles and gestured toward a chair. "Can you stay for a minute?" he said, smiling.

"You have quite a collection," I said, nodding toward the stack of books on his nightstand. Flannery O'Connor. Gore Vidal. Robertson Davies. Armistead Maupin. John Irving. Anne Rice. Margaret Atwood.

He nodded. "I've had a lot of time to read lately. If only I could stay awake long enough to finish a chapter."

"Terry said you were looking for a breviary and a missal. I'm afraid we don't have them here, but I'll bring them on Thursday," I said.

"You're Catholic?" he asked.

"Not anymore," I said, averting my gaze.

"If you're baptized, you're Catholic. Once a Catholic, always a Catholic." John patted my wrist, and I recoiled, knocking my elbow into the nightstand.

"I'm sorry," he said. "I didn't mean to offend."

"It's okay. It's nothing. I startle easily. I have to go anyway."

I hurried out the door and left without stopping at the office to say goodbye to Chris. I wanted to get home as quickly as possible. When John had touched my wrist, just above the scar on the back of my hand, I knew he didn't mean anything by it. I'd reacted badly. If I had learned anything from the residents at Neil's House, it was that people with AIDS were often treated like pariahs, even by their own families. But John's comment, *once a Catholic, always a Catholic*, had hit a nerve, and then his touch stung like a quick electric shock. I hadn't been able to stop myself from pulling away. I knew what Dr. LaRue would say, that it was important to set boundaries, that what I might see as overreaction was really self-preservation. Still, I felt guilty about what had happened. I couldn't shake the chill of regret. I took a long shower, then toweled off, and put on my warmest pair of pajamas. I was still cold, so I pulled on Neil's old cardigan, which turned out to be exactly the comfort I needed.

Rachel came by in the evenings when Sara worked the afternoon shift. She pretended to study: spread her books across the table, pulled her hair back in a ponytail, sharpened a few pencils onto a sheet of loose-leaf paper. Her posturing made no sense—she would have gotten more studying done alone in their quiet apartment—but I didn't suggest that to her. I loved having her there, loved knowing she was still *my* Rachel, at least some of the time. We sat at the table and drank tea, eventually shuffling the books and papers aside to make room for oatmeal cookies or lemon squares or another of my baking experiments. One evening, as we cut into a pan of brownies, Rachel picked up one of her textbooks. "Check this out," she said. "Phantom Limb Syndrome. It's something amputees get. Even though their arm or leg is gone, they still feel it like it's there. They can still sense pain or hot or cold in it. They know it's missing, but their brain tells them it's still attached. Isn't that the strangest thing?"

"Yeah, strange," I said, distracted. I took our cups to the kitchen and put the kettle on to brew another pot.

Rachel went home around eleven, and I stretched out on the couch. For years I had tried to rid my mind of the dark, painful memories from my childhood, tried to separate myself from them. But they were always there, as tangible as phantom limbs.

I would never be able to ignore the searing sparks and flashes of memory. The best I could do was to shield myself from their scorching white flare.

I brought the breviary and missal to Neil's House and asked Chris if she would take them to John.

"Sorry, I would, but I'm on the run. I have a meeting at the United Way office in about five minutes," Chris said as she rushed out the door. "I'll see you Friday, though. Dinner at six-thirty?"

"See you then." I stood in Chris's empty office, holding the books. I leaned into the hallway, looking for a nurse or another volunteer to deliver them. No one was around, so I squared my shoulders, then walked down the hall toward John's room. *It will be fine*, I told myself. I took a deep breath and knocked.

"You're an angel," he said. He held the books, one in each hand, and smiled widely. "I haven't used these in a while, but in the last few weeks, I've been wanting to reconnect with them."

"Glad I could help," I said, forcing a tight smile. "If you need anything else, just let one of the nurses know."

I was almost out the door when John said, "I want to apologize for the other day."

"It was nothing. I.... It's me. It happens. Enjoy the books."

"Wait," John said. "Just sit for a minute."

I pulled the chair away from the bed and perched on the edge of the seat. I folded my arms across my chest, hugging myself tightly. Whatever John had to say, I would hear him out and be done with it.

"The other day, when I said 'once a Catholic, always a Catholic....' That was insensitive of me. You've closed that door, and I get that. I do. I'm not trying to change your mind, believe me. It's just one of the beautiful things about faith is that you can close the door, but it's never locked. You can always open it and walk back through."

"I've gotta go," I said and rushed from the room. I heard John say "*Wait!*" but didn't look back. When I was safely outside, I allowed hot tears to brim and fall.

---

I told Dr. LaRue about my interactions with John. "I don't know why this bothered me so much. He's old, he's sick. He didn't mean anything by it."

Dr. LaRue raised an eyebrow. "But it did mean something, to you."

"He was just trying to smooth things over. I shouldn't have let it get to me. It's not like he was trying to hurt me."

"No, he wasn't. But his words brought back feelings and memories."

I looked out the window, avoiding her gaze. The past felt like a heavy backpack I carried with me everywhere. "Why can't I just let it go?"

Dr. LaRue explained repression. "We all do it," she reassured. "We put painful things out of mind. It's not a bad thing, under certain circumstances. It protects us. But eventually, the traumatic experiences we repress come out—in dreams, as illnesses, or as emotional crises."

"But yesterday, with John, I felt so much hatred. I felt like I was going to explode. I could have screamed or even hit someone. That's not like me," I said.

"It's not easy to predict triggers," she replied. "In your case, your trauma began when you were very young. You've held on to it for a long time. Have you ever known someone whose appendix burst? The bacterial infection from appendicitis builds up, and the appendix enlarges to the point where it ruptures. Sometimes, people experience pain for months ahead of time, but sometimes, it comes on suddenly. You want to get to the appendix before it ruptures, to prevent the infection from spreading. You can't ignore the symptoms."

"So all my memories could burst all over the place one day?"

"Well, we hope not," Dr. LaRue said, smiling. "But keeping the pressure down, knowing the indications of stress, is important. That's why we're here."

I sighed. "I'd rather have appendicitis."

Dr. LaRue laughed. "You're doing good work here. It's never easy, but you're doing all the right things."

After our session, I walked home the long way, through the park by the lake. I could hear Dr. LaRue's voice in my head: *You're doing all the right things.* I wanted to believe her, and immediately after a session, I usually did. The trick was to hold on to that belief longer than a few hours, to trust that it was there, even if I couldn't feel it.

On the far side of the park, I ran into a woman from the CASA group. I was immediately overwhelmed with shame for my poor attendance at the meetings. We exchanged *hello*s and *how-are-you*s like acquaintances, not at all like people who knew every detail about the sadistic violations that had been inflicted on the other's body. She didn't say anything about CASA. Maybe I was not the only one who had distanced myself from the group. I wanted to ask if she had stopped going too, and if so, whether it was an act of self-defense or self-loathing. I almost suggested we get coffee, but the moment passed.

The rest of the way home, I looked at everyone I saw through a dark, speculative lens. How many of us were out there, going about our day-to-day lives like walking land mines, ready to explode at any moment? What about that little girl in the yellow shorts? That woman walking the cocker spaniel? Those girls riding bicycles, their long hair whipping in the breeze? The parking garage attendant? The woman at the bus stop in the pale blue scrubs? All the women hurrying in and out of the grocery store—who among them was one of us? What about the children in their shopping carts and on their hips?

When I reached my building, I rode up in the elevator with a middle-aged woman in a floral print dress. She held a brown paper bag full of groceries, and I noticed her nails were bitten to the quick. When she got off at her floor, she smiled and said, "Have a nice day!"

I wanted to call after her, *You too? You too?*

I was kneeling beside the bookcase in the common room, shelving a few new titles, when John came up behind me and cleared his throat. "I didn't want to startle you," he said. "Can we talk?"

My first impulse was to make a dash for the front door and keep running as far as my lungs and legs would allow. Instead, I took a deep breath and told myself, *You can do this.*

I looked John in the eyes and said, "I have five minutes."

I set my work aside and sat on a nearby sofa, and John turned his walker around and sat on the seat. He was winded from walking down the hallway, and I waited while he caught his breath.

"Thank you again for the books," he said. "What you do here is.... You don't know what it means to me, to everyone here. I've been sick for almost four years, and I was alone most of the time. The care, the sense of community, it's made such a difference."

"I'm glad." I forced myself to hold his gaze. It was difficult, but I needed to hear what he had to say.

"I just...I wanted to apologize. Again. And, I'm not sure if I should say this, but after you left the other day, I realized who you are. I recognized you from the newspapers and TV, from the coverage of the court case."

Heat rushed up from my chest and colored my cheeks. I closed my eyes, willing them not to water.

John continued. "I knew that priest, years ago. Not very well. I was in the seminary."

My heart pounded and my hands began to sweat. I wanted to bolt, but I couldn't move. I opened my eyes and searched his face, pleading with him to let me go.

"I wasn't a priest," he said quickly. "I didn't stay in seminary. I figured out pretty early on that religious life wasn't for me. But I met him a few times. He was a young priest then, and he came to the sem to help with retreats. The faculty and priests who worked there held him up to us as an example. He'd been a model seminarian, one of their Golden Boys. But there was something about him that was off. And I'm not just saying that now—I said it then too. So did some of the other guys. I didn't know what had become of him, what kind of predator he was, but when I heard, I just felt sick."

I had been holding my breath, and I exhaled loudly. John continued.

"I guess I wanted to tell you, to be honest with you. I know we got off on the wrong foot, and I'm probably the last person you want to talk to. But, I wonder...I just can't help thinking, maybe we have something in common. It's not the same, but I know what it feels like to be on the outside, to be forced out. I mean, I don't miss it, really—the Church. But there's something about the loss, about having it taken from you."

I nodded. Despite what he said, that he didn't miss it, the Church seemed to hold a pull for him somehow. Still, I knew what he was trying to say. Like John, I knew what it was like to be on the outside. We'd both had things stolen from us. And like many of the residents who came through Neil's House, maybe John was trying to find a way to reconcile it all, knowing he probably didn't have much time. I had my whole life ahead of me, time to figure it out, as difficult as that might be.

We sat quietly for a while. The sounds of Neil's House echoed down the corridor—coughing from one room, soft blues music from another, the squeaky wheels of an IV pole, footsteps, laughter, the opening and closing of doors.

---

I was nervous when I went to tell Chris and Mila my news, though I wasn't exactly sure why. Maybe it was because I valued their opinions so much, or maybe because once I said it out loud, I would have to follow through on my decision. It had taken me a while to decide. I'd read pamphlets, made lists of the pros and cons, weighed my options. Once I had made my choice, I was excited to put my plan in place. And telling Chris and Mila was the first step.

I waited until after dinner, when Chris was clearing the table and Mila was pouring the last few drops of Chardonnay into her glass.

"I'm going back to school," I blurted.

Mila smiled widely and squeezed my upper arm. "That's wonderful!" she said. "I'm happy for you."

Chris sat down beside me. "That's great news. It's about time. Nursing? Oooh—or that new Public Health Education program they've started up at the college? You would be so good at that!"

"Not healthcare." I laughed, shaking my head. I'd known that's what she would think. "I'm going to try the Journalism program."

"*Really?*" Chris said. "I would never have thought.... Wait. Aren't you the person who called reporters *vultures*? Or was it *parasites*? Or maybe it was—"

"Alright, alright, I know. I admit—most of them are not my kind of people. I'm thinking more along the lines of long-form investigative journalism. I want to write about things that really matter, to tell the kinds of stories you don't usually see in the newspapers. At least, that's what I think I want to do. I guess I'll figure it out as I go."

"You will. I know you will," said Mila.

My eyes brimmed with tears, and I dabbed at them with my dinner napkin. Chris and Mila smiled at each other across the table.

All along, I had needed their support to help me find it in myself. Until that moment, I hadn't realized how much.

CASA planned a demonstration in front of the cathedral for the first Sunday in September, the day before the civil case brought by three of Father's victims was set to begin. The diocese had tried several tactics in order to delay. They claimed the Bishop was unwell, their lawyers needed more time to prepare, they were having difficulty locating pertinent documents. Finally, just a week before the trial date, the court granted their stay, and the date was moved into the next year. Victims' rights groups were irate. The media coverage was sympathetic to the women, and the story received wide publicity. CASA was determined to keep the attention on the victims, and even those of us who hadn't been going to meetings wanted to attend the rally to show our support.

The forecast for the day said rain, but the morning was bright, an early September day with the green of late summer but the crisp air of fall, the kind of day when even the most jaded turn their faces toward the sky like sunflowers, worshipping warmth and light. As I walked toward the cathedral, my JUSTICE FOR

VICTIMS sign over my shoulder, the anxiety I felt was tempered by determination. In the past, I'd dreaded public events. I still wasn't entirely comfortable, but I knew how important it was to show up. I'm not sure I could have articulated it in that moment, but there was something exhilarating about the power of women coming together, the strength of our collective voice.

When I arrived, I was surprised to see how many people were already assembled. Just a year before, we felt lucky when a dozen of us had shown up; now at least thirty protesters lined the sidewalk, maybe more. I merged with the silent crowd and started counting as more people arrived. A few parishioners hesitated when they reached the cathedral steps. I thought they would turn away, ignoring us as they had in the past, but instead they joined us. Before long we were fifty, fifty-five, sixty.

Mostly, I stared straight ahead as we walked back and forth, back and forth, back and forth. Then, something made me look at the cathedral entrance just as a short woman with light brown hair wearing a navy blue dress entered the cathedral. I couldn't be sure, but she looked like my mother. *It could be anyone*, I told myself. *Any brown-haired woman in a blue dress. Someone else. Someone else's mother.*

Just then, the opening chords of the processional hymn reached the street, and Rachel ran up beside me. "I'm here!" she said, a little too loudly. She looked at me and smiled. "Nice disguise."

I was wearing sunglasses and a baseball cap. "It's sunny. Give me a break. And lower your voice," I whispered, more harshly than I'd intended.

Rachel looked hurt. "Get up on the wrong side of the bed?"

I never snapped at Rachel. "Sorry. I'm just.... It's just...."

"Hey, it's okay," Rachel said as she linked her arm through mine.

We walked for about five minutes in silence. Finally, I said, "I think I saw Mom go into the cathedral. I know she still goes to mass, but how could she walk right past us? Past *me*? I'm probably wrong. I mean, I only saw her from behind. It could have been anyone." It was more a question than a comment.

Rachel sighed. "You could be right. You probably are." Rachel pulled me out of the line of protestors. We stood face to face on the cathedral's immaculately manicured lawn. She grasped my hands tightly. "I'd say she doesn't mean anything by it, but that wouldn't be true. But it doesn't mean what you think it means."

I couldn't bear to hear Rachel make excuses for her. I tried to pull away, but Rachel held on.

"Listen to me," Rachel said. "I think mom really believes praying, going to mass, saying the rosary and whatever, make a difference. She thinks everything will change, that things will go back to the way they were, and everything will be okay."

"But how could she walk right past us, past me?" I said again. "Don't defend her."

"I'm not. You know, I tried to come out to her—to her and Dad—a while ago. Just before Easter. I worked out what to say, practiced it a hundred times, and after dinner, I started telling them. And she didn't even let me finish. She just said something about how nice it was that I had a 'friend,' then went into the laundry room, and turned on the dryer."

"Rachel, I'm so sorry." All this time I thought Rachel and I were together in everything. And I'd missed this. "I didn't know."

"It's not your fault. It's not anybody's fault. That's what I'm trying to say. She really thinks she can pray it all away. It's messed up, but it's just the way it is. You can't change it. I know it's hard, but you just have to let it go. Put your energy into things that will actually make a difference."

We rejoined the line of protesters and walked for another half hour. I made excuses and left early, before mass ended. If it was my mother in the navy blue dress, I didn't want to see her when she exited. I knew I would have to face her eventually, but I would do it when I was ready, on my own terms.

I stopped a few blocks from home to pick up a cappuccino. The snug café's Sunday morning caffeine-and-sugar buzz seemed to have reached its peak. Every table was taken, and the conversations of the rejuvenated after-church crowd and the hungover morning-after crowd were indistinguishable. I took my order to go, and as I slipped my wallet back into my satchel, my hand grazed the portable tape recorder I'd purchased for my Introduction to Journalism course. I had been so excited when I bought it that I'd inserted the tiny cassette tape and batteries right away and put it in my satchel, even though classes didn't start until after Labor Day.

I crossed the street and sat at a picnic table in the park. I took the recorder out and hit record: *Testing one, two, three. Testing one, two, three.* I played it back and listened to my tinny voice. I pushed record again and began to speak. Just a few words. A long pause. And then a few more. And a few more. The words began to run together, at first in trickles and droplets, then as a narrow stream. Without warning, they gushed forth in a torrent, then subsided into a steady patter. *And then...and then...and then... and then....*

My story was long and winding. But I knew one day I would say, *And now....*

# [AFTERWORD]

The people, places, and events in *[non]disclosure* are fictional. Sadly, the broader subject matter is not.

In recent decades, cases of the sexual abuse of children by Roman Catholic priests have been tried in courts around the world in staggering numbers. Criminal and civil proceedings, as well as some of the out-of-court negotiations and financial settlements between victims and the larger institutional Church, have been reported extensively by television and print journalists. These cases have also inspired many documentary and feature films and novels.[1]

While writing *[non]disclosure*, I asked myself again and again, *Does the world really need another novel about such an abhorrent subject?* My answer, each time, was a decisive *YES*.

My rationale for writing about the sexual exploitation of girls in the context of institutional Roman Catholicism is threefold.

1 See reading list on p. 183.

First, female victims are underrepresented in works of fiction about the sexual abuse of children by priests. Although priest-pedophiles prey on both girls and boys, the majority of films and novels on the subject feature male protagonists (as both priests and victims). These works often rely on the trope of the defenseless altar boy, reinforcing stereotypes about male victims and vulnerability. A focus on lesser acknowledged female victims requires consideration of the gendered set of messages and behavioral expectations that are part and parcel of traditional Catholic girlhood. With *[non]disclosure*, I was keen to explore how ideas about Catholic girls' passivity, obedience, purity, virginity, and goodness affect the female victim and how she is perceived from childhood through young adulthood.

Further, many excellent novels explore the psychology of the priest-pedophile, but relatively few are told through the lens of the victim. I wanted to tell a story from a feminist perspective, taking care to honor the female victim by telling a story through *her eyes* and *her memory.*

My second motivation for writing *[non]disclosure* comes from bearing witness to how one particular case of serial sexual abuse by a Roman Catholic priest affected the community I call home. In 2006, the small city of Chatham, Ontario, made international headlines when Father Charles Sylvestre was convicted of sexually assaulting forty-seven victims over almost five decades as a parish priest in Chatham and the nearby communities of Windsor, Sarnia, London, and Pain Court, all in the Diocese of London, Ontario. Sylvestre's victims were between the ages of seven and fifteen years when they were abused; at the time of the court case, the youngest victim was thirty-two years old, and the oldest was sixty-four.[2]

It seemed that everyone in Chatham knew someone affected by the case, whether directly or indirectly. Every coffee

2 *From Isolation to Action, Child Sexual Abuse by Clergy: Managing a Major Case, R vs. Sylvestre*, From Isolation to Action Committee, editors (Bulldog Design, 2008), p. 8.

shop and diner, every workplace and social gathering, buzzed with discussions about the trial. Many people expressed sympathy and concern for the women victims, but others doubted their claims. Sylvestre had been a trusted religious authority in local churches for decades, had married hundreds of couples, baptized their children, buried their beloved family members. "Father Charlie," some people insisted, was "a nice guy." They couldn't—or wouldn't—see him for the serial predator he was, and they denounced women victims for their accusations.

I was sad and angry in equal parts. I didn't grow up in Chatham, so I didn't have the same connection to the case as those who had attended local schools and churches, and I am not a victim of abuse, but it affected me, nonetheless. I reached a point where I couldn't bring myself to discuss the subject. Then the writer in me said, *Listen. Write.* At the time, I was a columnist for the *Catholic New Times*, a Toronto-based, left-leaning, social justice paper. So, I listened. And I listened some more. And then I wrote. I published two columns, one about how the language we use when discussing sexual abuse by priests affects our ways of thinking about the cases,[3] and another reporting on the Bishop's public apology to the local church communities.[4] I knew there was much more to say, not only about the Sylvestre case but also about the experiences of victims and how their stories are regulated through public criticism, self-censure, and nondisclosure agreements.

Almost two decades have passed since the Sylvestre trial.[5] Of course, its conclusion did not end the suffering of victims.

3 Renée Bondy, "On Sexual Abuse, Institutional Language and Gender Inequality," *Catholic New Times* (Toronto, November 26, 2006).

4 Renée Bondy, "These Women Will Not Be Silenced," *Catholic New Times* (Toronto, September 24, 2006).

5 Sylvestre, who was eighty-four years old, was sentenced to a penitential term of three years. He died of natural causes while in prison.

The trauma of abuse suffered in childhood, compounded by court proceedings and subsequent civil litigation, has been devastating for victims and their families. Some suffer silently and anonymously. Others have endured further public scrutiny due to ongoing legal struggles with the Diocese of London.[6]

This tragedy has also affected the larger community. It has divided families and communities, fostered mistrust of the institutional Church, and triggered crises of faith in many lifelong Catholics. In some small way, I hope *[non]disclosure* provides insight into victims' experiences and promotes awareness, understanding, and empathy.

A third impetus for writing *[non]disclosure* is my belief that writers can and do make contributions to the pursuit of justice. Stories entertain, yes, but they also have the power to inform, educate, and challenge readers. When I consider my own history as a reader, I marvel at the ways books by my favorite authors have moved me and expanded my way of thinking about matters large and small. I think of how Richard Wagamese's *Indian Horse* contributes to a meaningful national conversation about residential schools, how Joy Kogawa's *Obasan* exposes the persecution and internment of Japanese Canadians during WWII, how Margaret Atwood's *The Handmaid's Tale* sparks discussion about the politicization and exploitation of women's bodies, how Joshua Whitehead's *Jonny Appleseed* offers insight into the Indigiqueer experience. These are just a few award-winning examples from a long list of Canadian authors whose writing prompts critical thinking and dialogue.

6 For example, in 2021, the case of *Irene Deschenes vs. the Diocese of London* went before the Supreme Court of Canada. Deschenes sought to reopen her civil case against the Diocese when documentation came to light indicating that the Diocese had known about Father Charles Sylvestre's history of predatory sexual behavior but denied this knowledge when an earlier case was settled with Deschenes in 2000. The Supreme Court ruled in favor of Deschenes, denying the Diocese's appeal and allowing Deschenes to reopen the case. See Kate Dubinski, "Supreme Court sides with London, Ont., woman suing Catholic church," *CBC News*, February 11, 2021.

My hope is that *[non]disclosure* will move readers to think deeply about the vulnerability of children, the abuse of power in patriarchal, hierarchical religious institutions, and the importance of speaking truth to power.

# [ACKNOWLEDGMENTS]

First and foremost, thank you to my partner, Tracy. Her enthusiastic encouragement, careful reading, thoughtful feedback, and loving support have been essential to *[non]disclosure.* This book would not be complete without her. I would not be complete without her.

Thank you to the team at Second Story Press: Margie Wolfe, Jordan Ryder, Phuong Truong, Emma Rodgers, April Masongsong, Laura Atherton, Michaela Stephen, and Kate Earnshaw for their dedication to *[non]disclosure* and for proving, book by book, that feminist presses play an essential role in the publishing landscape. Endless gratitude to Liz Johnston, a writer's dream editor, for her razor-sharp skill, deft touch, and sensitivity with the manuscript.

While writing *[non]disclosure,* I was mentored by the incomparable Diane Schoemperlen. Her guidance and belief in this story have meant the moon. Thank you to the Humber School for Writers, especially Director Alissa York. Early sections of *[non]disclosure* found rhythm in the Collegeville Institute for

Ecumenical Research and Writing's November 2020 *Writing Spirit, Writing Faith* workshop, expertly facilitated by Mary Potter. Tentative first pages were written in early fall of 2020 at the home of Rex Lingwood and Wendy Mitchinson. Wendy's praise of my writing, right from the start, has been a guiding light, and she is greatly missed.

My talented writing group, Gord, André, Danielle, Kim Conklin, and Doug, have made me a better writer in every way.

Jennifer Grant, Penni Mitchell, André Narbonne, Jane Nicholas, Danielle Price, Hollie Sparling, and Bruce Tucker read early bits and drafts of *[non]disclosure*. I am forever grateful for their generosity of time and expertise. Thanks to Karl Jirgens for his advice regarding publishing.

For the meaningful conversations that inspired *[non]disclosure*, some short, some long, some recent, some in the distant past, *thank you* to Ayesha Mian Akram, Kelly-Anne Appleton, Cindy Bonvarlez, Denise and Brian Donais, Kathleen Kevany, Mary T. Malone, Jane Nicholas, Danielle Price, Dennis O'Mara, Cheryl Robinson, Michelle Schryer, Charlene Senn, Christina Simmons, and Meredith Smye.

I am fortunate to have wonderfully supportive friends and family members. My love and gratitude to you all. Thank you to the Bondy and Bonvarlez families for their support, especially Dick and Denise Bondy and Pat and Frank Bonvarlez. And a special shout-out to my niece, Lorrayne, who loves a good book as much as I do.

# [READING LIST]

## Fiction

Andrew M. Greeley, *The Priestly Sins*, Forge Books, 2004.
Brendan Kiely, *The Gospel of Winter*, Margaret K. McElderry Books, 2014.
Jennifer Haigh, *Faith*, HarperCollins, 2011.
John Boyne, *A History of Loneliness*, Doubleday, 2014.
Linden MacIntyre, *The Bishop's Man*, Random House Canada, 2009.
Roddy Doyle, *Smile*, Jonathan Cape, 2017.
Sebastian Barry, *Old God's Time*, Viking, 2023.
Thomas Keneally, *Crimes of the Father*, Atria Books, 2017.

## Poetry

Mary Ann Mulhern, *When Angels Weep*, Black Moss Press, 2008.

## Memoir

Lacy Crawford, *Notes on a Silencing*, Little, Brown and Company, 2020.

## Nonfiction

*From Isolation to Action, Child Sexual Abuse by Clergy: Managing a Major Case, R. vs. Sylvestre*, ed. FITA Committee, Bulldog Design, Inc., 2008.

Jim Gilbert, *Breach of Faith, Breach of Trust: The Story of Lou Ann Soontiens, Father Charles Sylvestre, and Sexual Abuse within the Catholic Church*, iUniverse Inc., 2009.

## Documentary Films

*Deliver Us from Evil*, directed by Amy Berg (Disarming Films, 2006).

*The Keepers*, directed by Ryan White (Netflix, 2017).

*Prey*, directed by Matt Gallagher (Border City Pictures Inc., 2019).

*Procession*, directed by Robert Greene (Netflix, 2021).

## Feature Films

*The Boys of St. Vincent*, directed by John N. Smith (National Film Board of Canada, 1992).

*Doubt*, directed by John Patrick Shanley (Miramax Films, 2008).

*The Magdalene Sisters*, directed by Peter Mullan (Momentum Pictures, 2002).

*Spotlight*, directed by Tom McCarthy (Open Road Films, 2016).

# [ABOUT THE AUTHOR]

**Renée D. Bondy** is a writer and educator. A longtime contributor to *Herizons* magazine, her writing has also appeared in *Bearings Online*, *Bitch*, and the *Humber Literary Review*, and her essays have been featured on CBC Radio. Renée holds degrees in Religious Studies and History, including a PhD in History from the University of Waterloo (2007). She taught in the Women's and Gender Studies program at the University of Windsor for several years, where she facilitated courses on queer activism, women and religion, and the history of women's movements.

Renée is a graduate of the Humber School for Writers. When she is not sitting at the keyboard, Renée is an avid swimmer, baker, cruciverbalist, and hospice volunteer. Renée and her partner live in Chatham, Ontario. *[non]disclosure* is her first novel.